THE MENTOR

her. She's read everyon... and weekly visits to her local library to... of the New York Times and the New Yorker were... forting rituals. Finding a copy of the Post... rld stories of crime, depravity, and glamour ma... addition to the abstract expressionists, the A... Factory, she knows all about Son of Sam and K... edda Nussbaum. Emma has spent much of the last... rom one end of town to the other until she reach... rload and struggles back to her room to collaps... The sounds, the lights, the people, the motion... thing and thrilling. It's the anonymity that c... t she can move about unnoticed, released at la... inds. Sick evil minds. She's free; her desti... ead, around the next corner. It's getting dark o... close the city. The lights from the stores b... People stroll along, laughing and relaxed,... looks as if it's been airlifted in from Las Ve... fronted by a circular glass-walled lounge th... lled with tourists enjoying their first drink... f smugness Emma realizes that she isn't a touri... a job. And it isn't some boring automaton job... ce, but a job working for a famous businesswo... hat hums with creativity. Ha-ha! food all tho... onville. And her good fortune is no accident... he city's best employment agencies. She took... y Junior College. Knowing she would need a ref... ll summer at that insurance agency. She prep... job at Roseanne Turner's chic catalogue a... she stays late every night, poking around the... tails, organizing computer files. Even though... orary, it may well pay off. One thing leads to... e money she saved over the summer and start... l apartment. ...she looks around her at... he's where she belongs, in th... nows. "Hello!..."

THE MENTOR

Sebastian Stuart

BANTAM BOOKS
New York   Toronto   London   Sydney   Auckland

The author wishes to thank Ann Collette, Helen Rees, Joan Mazmanian, Audrey Schulman, and Stephen McCauley. And especially my editor, Beverly Lewis.

THE MENTOR

A Bantam Book / November 1999

BOOK DESIGN BY GLEN M. EDELSTEIN

Library of Congress Cataloging-in-Publication Data
Stuart, Sebastian.
The mentor / Sebastian Stuart.
p. cm.
ISBN 0-553-11165-5
I. Title.
PS3569.T827M46   1999
813'.54—dc21   98-51447
                                                            CIP

Published simultaneously in the United States and Canada

Bantam Books are published by Bantam Books, a division of Random House, Inc. Its trademark, consisting of the words "Bantam Books" and the portrayal of a rooster, is Registered in U.S. Patent and Trademark Office and in other countries. Marca Registrada. Bantam Books, 1540 Broadway, New York, New York 10036.

PRINTED IN THE UNITED STATES OF AMERICA
BVG   10 9 8 7 6 5 4 3 2 1

In memory of S.L.

THE MENTOR

NEW YORK IS EMMA'S obsession. And so when she gets off work she decides to walk back to the YMCA on West Twenty-third Street where, since her arrival in the city a month earlier, she's been living in a dingy little room that smells faintly of mildew. She walks across Fifty-fourth Street to Seventh Avenue and turns south—up ahead she can see Times Square's neon bazaar beckoning like a fun house barker.

It's a warm, cloudy evening; the sky is low and a darkening gray; the humid air seems to leach the smells out of the city: food, humanity, concrete, a heady, seductive brew laced with a trace of the sea. Emma thought she knew everything about New York, but the smells surprise and tantalize her. She's read everyone from Edith Wharton to Tom Wolfe, and weekly visits to her local library to pore over the latest issues of the *New York Times* and the *New Yorker* were one of her childhood's few comforting rituals. Finding a copy of the *Post* was a special pleasure—its lurid stories of crime, depravity, and glamour made her yearn for the city. In addition to the abstract expressionists, the Actors Studio, Warhol and the Factory, she knows all about Son of Sam and Kitty Genovese, sex clubs and Hedda Nussbaum.

Emma has spent much of the last month walking, just walking from one end of town to the other until she reaches the point of sensory overload and straggles back to her room to collapse on the narrow, lumpy bed. The sounds, the lights, the people, the motion—she finds the cacophony both soothing and thrilling. It's the anonymity that comforts her most, the sense that she can move about unnoticed, released at last from the scrutiny of evil minds. Sick evil minds. She's free: her destiny might be waiting just up ahead, around the next corner.

It's getting dark out, a darkness that seems to enclose the city. The lights from the stores bathe Broadway in a warm glow. People stroll along, laughing and relaxed. Emma passes a hotel tower that looks as if it's been airlifted in from Las Vegas. Snazzy and brazen, it's fronted by a circular glass-walled lounge the size of a bus depot that's filled with tourists enjoying their first drink of the evening. With a touch of smugness Emma realizes that she isn't a tourist. She lives here. She has a job. And it isn't some boring automaton job in some fluorescent-lit office, but a job working for a famous businesswoman—Anne Turner—in an office that hums with creativity. Ha-ha! Fuck all those pieces of shit back in Munsonville. And her good fortune is no accident. No way. Emma researched the city's best employment agencies. She took a computer course at Allegheny Junior College. Knowing she would need a reference, she worked diligently all summer at that insurance agency. She prepared herself. And when the job at *Home*—Anne Turner's chic catalog—came along, she grabbed it, and now she stays late every night, poking around the office, taking care of tiny details, organizing computer files. Even though the job is officially only temporary, it may well pay off. One thing leads to another.

Now Emma can take the money she saved over the summer and start to hunt for an apartment, a real apartment. She looks around her at the teeming avenue and feels as if she's where she belongs, in this city where she has no past. Where nobody knows.

"Hello!"

Emma turns. A woman wearing a dark business suit takes her wrist. Emma tries to pull away but the woman holds fast.

"I know you," the woman says, tilting her head and examining Emma with huge brown eyes. Emma notices the suit has a food stain on it and the collar is frayed. The woman leans in and Emma smells something foul—a mix of sour whiskey, ancient sweat, and madness. Emma knows that smell. She shudders and tries to pull away. The woman tightens her grip. Emma looks around wildly. No one is paying any attention; people are walking, walking so quickly. Are they trying to get away?

"I know you. Don't pretend you don't know me."

"Let go, please."

"Why should I? I know you." The woman twists Emma's wrist and all the people stream by and the woman's mouth is open and she flicks her tongue like a lizard and Emma takes a step backward and the woman twists her wrist harder and just keeps coming at her.

Then Emma shoves her, hard, just shoves that filthy, horrible woman back, hard, and it's the last thing the woman is expecting and her mouth flies open in shock and she lets go of Emma's wrist and loses her balance and falls down on the sidewalk. She starts to say something—something vile and inhuman and evil—and Emma takes a step toward her and the woman shuts up, but she lifts her chin and smooths her filthy hair as if she's Jackie fucking Onassis and Emma is beneath her station.

Emma wants to bring her foot up under that filthy chin and kick that jaw shut and teach that woman to go around grabbing people who're minding their own business. She wants to hurt her. Emma is frightened by what she wants. She mumbles "I'm sorry" and rushes away—and the memory comes back, the memory always comes back. BadGirlSickGirl. As Emma hurries down the street, away from the memory, she feels the sidewalk drop out from beneath her, she feels the city suddenly grow flat, she feels the rage and hopelessness that dwell—covered, caged, denied—at the core of her being. She only wants to go back, back to her room.

Emma sits by the grimy window in the grimy room, looking out at the air shaft. All her lights are out and she can see into other rooms across the way. They're all empty. Emma hates herself for pushing that woman. She lost her cool—she can't lose her cool, not here, not in New York. This is her new life. It's going to work out for her here. It has to, it *has* to. BadGirlSickGirl. Emma holds out her arm and looks at the expanse of pale flesh. She opens her secret box, the tiny tin box painted with flowers long faded. Inside is the worn red velvet she loves so much. She lifts the velvet and there it is—her friend. She runs her fingertip over the smooth metal of the single-edge razor blade. So cool and soothing.

There's a loud knock on her door.

Emma freezes.

"Jo-ey!" a drunken voice calls.

Emma sits absolutely still.

"Open up, ya dumb fuck!"

The drunk rattles the door handle. He slams his palm against the door and mutters, "Asshole."

Emma listens as the footfalls retreat. She switches on the light. She isn't going to end up like that, lurching down hallways in depressing old rooming houses. Fuck that shit. She picks up her box and for a moment considers throwing it out the window. She folds the red velvet over the razor blade and puts the box in her top drawer. Then she sits down at the small desk and gets to work.

1

CHARLES IS RUNNING. Usually he runs around the reservoir once, maybe twice, but today he doesn't want to stop, he wants to push himself. After his second time around, he jogs down the path and onto West Drive and keeps running. It's early afternoon, the day is chilly, it looks as if it's going to rain. He can't remember the last time he ran this far, he's sweating heavily in spite of the chill and his lungs burn as he sucks down oxygen, but he doesn't want to stop, he wants to run, high on hope.

He thinks of Anne. They've been so distant lately, both preoccupied with their careers. Even their lovemaking is perfunctory. They shouldn't have bought the apartment. They overreached and they know it. Land mines of resentment dot the marriage. He hasn't been pulling his weight financially, has been distracted, irritable. Yes, envious. But that's all about to change.

Charles runs past a playground. In the distance he can hear faint strains of the carousel's calliope music. He grimaces as a sudden stitch knots his side. Age—it scares him. That low back pain that flares up after a long drive, the eyestrain after an hour at the computer, the inexorable retreat of his hairline—there's no doubt his body is starting to betray him. He picks up his pace.

The party for *Capitol Offense* is on Wednesday. The book has been in the stores for a week. He has a good feeling about this one. The publishing world has been ignoring him lately. It's all cyclical, though, and after the last two disappointments, he's due for a measure of the success and respect his earlier books received. He's earned it. Through some confluence of good fortune, DeLillo, Banks, and Ford are all absent from this fall's lists. There's room for him at the top. Again, after all these years.

He nears the northern end of the park, where Harlem begins. A few heavy raindrops start to fall. The park is emptying out quickly. A wind comes up, damp and cold. He runs past a wide green lawn interrupted by outcroppings of gray bedrock, like whales rising from the sea. Charles tries to ignore the blister he feels opening on his left foot. He's in great shape. Isn't he? How many forty-nine-year-old men can run like this, just keep running? He has stamina, staying power. His best years are yet to come. After things settle down, he'll lavish attention on Anne, make amends for his recent moodiness. She's been so understanding.

The rain picks up, the drops coming quicker. When he was in his twenties, he loved to run in the rain. He can still handle it. It's wilder up in the northern reaches of the park; there are patches of trees that look like deep woods. He passes two black girls huddled under an overpass, making out, their passion stoked by the veil of rain. It's coming down steadily now, blown by gusts of wind. Charles's sweatshirt is soaked.

And then his cell phone rings and he takes it out of his belly pack. Anne says it's embarrassingly Hollywood of him to take calls while he's running.

"Ray's Pizza," he says.

"I'd like a large pie with pepperoni and pineapple."

Charles laughs. It's Nina, his agent. More important, his friend for over twenty years.

"Where the hell are you, Charles?"

"Somewhere in Central Park, partner. Swimming against the current."

"In this rain? Thank God the exercise bug never bit me. Call me when you get in."

Charles can hear something serious in her voice—they know each other that well. He ducks under a tree, his body heaving with each breath.

"What have you got for me?" he asks.

"A disappointment, I'm afraid. Call me later."

"Better tell me now, Nina. I like to be wet when I get bad news."

"Well, I just saw an advance copy of the *Times Book Review*."

Charles crouches down and leans back against the tree.

"And?"

"Some envious hack takes out his frustrations on you."

Charles hears a high-pitched screech but there's no ambulance, no police car.

"Charles, are you there?"

"Who wrote it?" he asks, ready to add another name to the enemies list.

Nina mentions someone who sounds vaguely familiar. One of those writing-program one-novel wonders?

"How bad is it, on a scale of one to ten?"

"You don't need to read this one, Charles."

"I'll call you later."

"Listen to me, Charles—"

"I'm going to hang up now, Nina. Good-bye."

Charles stands up and starts to run back downtown. Faster. By the end of the day, every publisher and agent in the city will have read that review. When he gets home, he has to call Anne and tell her. He can just hear the sympathy in her voice. The concern that masks her pity.

And then he falls—trips over himself, crashes down on his right knee, scraping flesh off his knee and his palm. He picks himself up and keeps running, ignoring the pain and the blood. He's nearing Seventy-second Street, his route home. He splashes through a rush of water pouring down a storm drain. His running shoes are soaked and he has to blink to see through the downpour. He's been counting on a good paperback sale from this one. Something in the mid six figures. The *Times* review probably lopped an easy hundred grand off that. He can't ask Little Miss Success to take up the slack, as if he were a kept husband. He imagines, for one brief troubling instant, hitting Anne, slapping the concern off that exquisite face. His knee and palm are pulsing with pain. He sees his apartment building rising above the trees. He runs right past it and keeps on running.

2

ANNE TURNER IS in her office going over the copy for the spring catalog. She's having trouble concentrating. Outside, the rain is coming down in sheets. She's a California girl; rain this fierce scares her; it brings mud slides—houses, dreams, lives that once seemed solid and secure, all swept away in an instant.

She signs off on a rhapsodic description of wrought-iron furniture made at a small foundry outside Florence, gets up and paces for a moment, then pours herself another cup of coffee—her fourth so far today. Damn Trent for being on vacation. She can always count on her assistant to cheer her up with some juicy bit of celebrity gossip. That mousy little temp the agency sent over looks like she wouldn't know gossip from wheatgrass.

Everything is so infuriatingly unsettled right now. She's never told Charles how precarious her position is. How could she, after insisting that they buy the apartment? Yes, in three brief years, *Home* had become one of the most popular catalogs in the country, but costs are astronomical. Her insistence on scouring the globe for sensational offerings, on using the most expensive paper, on hiring the best photographers, on leasing these lavish thirty-fourth-floor offices, have all stretched resources to the breaking point. There's a little breathing room now, thank God, but only because she took drastic action—action that makes her shudder every time she thinks of it.

Anne hates the way Charles has been sulking over every minor setback and disguising his envy of her growing fame. So much is at stake with his new book, and she's afraid his expectations are unrealistically high. It's a good book, but not his best, not as good as it could be, *should* be, with his gift. Damn, she hates it when she pities him. What she should do right this second is kick off her shoes and do ten minutes of yoga. But the truth is, yoga bores the hell out of her. Work is the only thing that releases her endorphins.

Anne adores the gargoyle planters made by some mad old hippie deep in the Joshua Tree desert—they're terrifying, fabulous, and unique. Just the sort of find that has made *Home* such a sensation. The coffee is starting to make her dizzy. Her phone lights up.

"Your husband is on line one, Ms. Turner," the temp says in her tentative voice.

Anne punches on the speaker.

"Are you warm and dry, darling?" Silence from the other end of the line. What now? "Charles?"

"It's the *Times Book Review*."

"Not good?"

"Not even so-so."

For a split second Anne fears she'll faint. She looks out the window at the furious storm—is the whole city coming apart? Pity won't do; she knows that.

"Who wrote it?" she asks.

"Does it matter?"

"We can discredit him. Call in all our chits. Make sure someone sympathetic writes the daily *Times* review."

There's a pause and she can tell Charles is considering her idea.

Anything to keep him from spiraling down into that morbid depression of his, the one that shrouds the apartment like cobwebs. The one that eventually winds itself around her throat, too.

"It's one review, Charles," she says. "It's a goddamn good book and we both know it. And you're a great writer." She realizes that in some perverse way she welcomes his crisis. At least now she has something to latch on to, a challenge. And if she can help him through this, an atonement.

"I just wanted to let you know."

"Let's go out to dinner tonight—get drunk and feel each other up under the table."

"Great idea. How about the Four Seasons? To complete the humiliation, why don't I walk in naked?"

Anne curses herself. There is simply no way to minimize the blow—the *Times Book Review* is Big Daddy.

"I love you," she says. "I can't wait to get home."

Anne goes to the window. Down below, the city is a wet gray blur.

The intercom sounds. "Ms. Turner, may I speak to you a moment, please?"

The mouse squeaks, Anne thinks.

"What is it?"

The temp enters. She's small and young and quite pretty, actually, when she lets her face peek out from the unruly brown hair that keeps falling down from behind her ears. Large green eyes, lovely skin, a mouth that could be sensual if she'd let it.

"In these catalog pages that you okayed?"

"Yes?"

"I found two errors."

"You're kidding me." Anne takes fierce pride in her attention to detail.

"See the extra space between the period and the start of the next sentence here? And 'pâté' needs an acute accent over the *e*."

The last thing most temps will do is take it upon themselves to review the boss's work.

"You've got a good eye, Edna."

The phone rings.

"I'll get it myself. . . . Anne Turner."

"Anne, it's Judith Arnold."

Her gynecologist. Anne stiffens.

"The test is in. Hope you and Charles have some champagne on ice."

"You're positive?"

"No doubt. You're going to have a baby."

Anne can feel the blood rush from her head and then, just as quickly, her face flushes hot red. She sits in a gray chair she's never sat in before. Christ, she wishes the rain would let up; she can't think through its splattery tattoo. And she needs to think.

"It's Emma."

She's forgotten that the young woman is still in the room. "What?"

"My name. It's not Edna, it's Emma."

"Thank you, Emma. Hold all calls."

When the girl is gone, Anne looks out the window again. But now all she can see is her own reflection, staring back at her with fear and contempt.

3

ANNE STRIDES DOWN the cavernous hallway of the Central Park West apartment in her bra, panties, and the new Manolo Blahnik heels she paid six hundred dollars for at Bergdorf's. She hates heels, they're uncomfortable and send the wrong message. But today is a heels day—some days just are. Anne has spent the last week in a state of low-level panic. She called Judith Arnold back and swore her to secrecy about the pregnancy. She also asked for some pills to quell her anxiety, but was told they all carried too many risks. Anne reminds herself constantly how important it is to keep going. The next couple of weeks are going to be about Charles and the book. After that, she'll have time to think. To decide.

She and Charles have been moving through the house as if in parallel universes. He began to slip down that black hole of his, but then, to his credit, he started work on a short story to take his mind off things. He's also running compulsively, for hours at a time, and then polishing off two bottles of wine during their tense, desultory dinners. Anne knows that the less she says the better—they just have to wait and see how the release of *Capitol Offense* plays out. She yearns for the connection and release of lovemaking, but Charles loses all interest in sex when he's depressed or resentful and right now he's both.

In the kitchen—the kitchen that recently graced the pages of *Metropolitan Home*—Anne digs into the perfectly ripe papaya half Magdalena has left, as per instructions, on the bare white vastness of the room's center island. Anne adores papaya—fat free, good for the digestion, and when perfectly ripe it literally melts on the tongue. Fifty percent of eating is texture, the other fifty percent is guilt. She looks around the gleaming room with its glass-front cabinets. None of that au courant clutter for her, thank you very much. The mania for baskets—woven grease-magnets she calls them—sets her teeth on edge. Anne is glad they bought the apartment, in spite of the squeeze it has put them in. She loves the space, the light, the views. In the past year their dinner parties have become coveted invitations, in no small part because people want to see what Anne Turner has done in her *own* home.

Anne listens. Beyond the door—the door that leads to Charles's domain, the chaotic domain of Charles Davis—she hears nothing. She never does, although that never stops her from listening.

The kitchen phone rings.

"Yes."

"Good morning, darling."

Anne runs her fingers through her hair—this is the last person she wants to talk to today.

"Hello, Mother."

"You didn't answer my E-mail."

"I've been swamped. Where are you?"

"Palm Beach. Did you forget? Tory Clarke's wedding is this weekend. You were invited."

"I'd rather book a root canal than go to Tory Clarke's wedding. She's as narrow-minded and right wing as the rest of her family."

Damn! Ten seconds into the call and she's already regressed from successful thirty-six-year-old to hostile teenager. Her earliest memory is of her mother dragging her to riding lessons, telling her she was going to win a gold medal in the Olympics. Then there were the French lessons, the dancing class, the B-minus in math that cost her the class trip to Catalina.

"Is everything all right, Anne?"

Anne can imagine Frances—who's on her second face-lift and third husband—flushed from her morning workout, perched on the edge of a chaise in the guest suite of some friend's mansion, sipping tea off the tray the maid delivered, looking out at the ocean, and patting on $100-an-ounce under-eye cream.

"I sent Tory a present. Give her my best. How are you and Dwight?" Anne's current stepfather is a real estate developer who rode the southern California population boom straight to the Forbes 400. Her real father, an aeronautical engineer whom Anne adored, died of cancer when she was eight years old. His death bewildered and terrified her and left her with a haunting fear that the worst always happens, a fear she denies, even to herself.

"We're wonderful, although Palm Beach is awfully humid. Why does anyone live on the East Coast? Listen, darling, I just wanted to check in and see how Charles's new book is doing. We're all breathless with anticipation."

Frances Allen has never really approved of Charles, and Anne is sure she'd like nothing better than for the new book to fail. She groomed her daughter to marry a titan of industry, someone with serious money, places in Bel Air and Pebble Beach, private planes and entrée into the highest levels of government. Not some novelist who's part of the condescending East Coast cultural elite.

"The book is doing well," Anne says.

"Have any reviews come out?"

"No," Anne lies.

"Then how do you know it's doing well?"

Anne takes a deep breath.

"I've got a big day, Mom."

"I don't doubt it."

"Give my best to Dwight."

"Listen, darling, we're going to be in New York next month. Or at least *I* am. You know how your stepfather feels about that city. I'll be at the Plaza Athénée."

"Let me know the dates. Good-bye, Mother."

Anne hangs up and immediately scoops out the rest of the papaya. The call was par for the course—not one question about *Home*, about how Anne is doing. Frances is a raging narcissist who sees her own life in color and everyone else's in black-and-white. She hates her daughter for being younger and prettier than she is, for forging a career that eclipses Frances, for— Stop it! Anne has no time for those old tapes. Not today. Not ever.

Suddenly the door to Charles's office flies open. Anne gasps.

"Jesus, Charles, you scared me."

Charles storms through the kitchen. Anne puts down the papaya and counts to fifteen. Then she heads toward the back of the apartment. In spite of everything, she's excited by Charles—what woman wouldn't be?

She stands in the bathroom doorway watching as he splashes cold water on his face over and over again.

"I take it your work didn't go well this morning?"

"No need to 'take it.' Why don't you just ask me?"

Uh-oh, impossible mood.

Anne crosses the bedroom, past the bank of windows that look out over the park, walks into her closet, and grabs two dresses, two short (but not too short), sexy dresses—what's the point of chiseling down her thighs if she doesn't show them off—one deep red, one this marvelous metallic shade of burnt gold.

"Charles, which one should I wear tonight? I want to look like a trophy wife."

That gets a smile out of him. He looks from the dresses to her body.

"The gold."

He's right, of course—the dress's tawny gleam sets off her red hair and pale, freckle-splashed skin to high advantage. Anne hooks the dress on the back of the door. She quietly slips into her slacks and blouse. Charles sits brooding on the edge of the mahogany sleigh bed.

Anne sits beside him and rubs his neck.

"You know how much I believe in you, darling. We'll get through all this."

He turns to her, looking so vulnerable, so vulnerable and so gorgeous, with that full mouth, those hazel eyes cradled in their comforting web of wrinkles, that tousled chestnut hair, that jaw covered with stubble, bristly stubble that brings an exciting hint of pain when it moves across her flesh.

"Oh, Anne, I didn't marry an optimist for nothing."

And he kisses her, lightly, on the lips. Anne knows that in many ways she's stronger than Charles. He's an artist—certain critics have even called him a genius—prey to unspeakable demons, crippling doubts. His work is so important. Sometimes, late at night when she can't sleep, Anne will tiptoe into the library, pick up one of his books, and reread a favorite passage. What compelling characters he creates, how beautifully he puts words together, capturing all the pain and frailty and radiance of life. And this man loves *her*. She wants so much to help him right now, for his sake, of course, but also, she admits to herself, to assuage her guilt over her success—and her transgression.

"Thanks for putting up with me, tea biscuit," he whispers in her ear.

"Hey, no problem."

"You be the best."

"I had a silly idea," Anne says tentatively.

"We should take off for Bangkok?"

"I wish we could. If you hate the idea just say so, but do you think maybe it would help if you got your office organized? Just a little."

He refuses to let the housekeeper enter the rooms where he works, the former maids' quarters down that long hallway off the kitchen. Anne, organized to a fault, is secretly appalled by the unanswered mail, unreturned phone calls, unfiled papers. She's sure a clean sweep would help Charles stay focused on the future, on his new work.

"I relent. Magdalena can haul in the Dirt Devil and work her magic."

"But what about cleaning out some of the deadwood? I had this fantastic temp last week while Trent was on vacation. Completely unobtrusive. Why don't I call the agency and have them send her over? If you don't like having her around, we'll send her right back."

Charles walks into the bathroom and turns on the sauna. Anne follows.

"Will you at least consider it?" she asks.

"I will."

"HG-TV is coming up to the office this afternoon to shoot a piece on *Home*, so I won't see you till the party. What time is your *Book Talk* taping?"

"They're sending a car at four-thirty," Charles says, taking off his shirt and slipping out of his pants. There he is in those striped boxers, with that boxer build—a boxer gone slightly, sexily to seed.

"Nina's expecting a mob scene," Anne says, her gaze running down his body.

"Free food'll do it every time." Charles steps out of his shorts. Anne catches her breath. She looks at the two of them in the mirror. Their eyes meet. He looks wounded, wary. She wants him so badly but is afraid of being rebuffed, of adding to the distance between them. She crosses to him and kisses him, putting a hand on his chest. He accepts her kiss passively.

"I'll see you this evening," she says. "And do think about the girl. I think she might be a help."

4

"WELCOME TO *BOOK TALK*. I'm Derek Wollman, and my guests today are Charles Davis and Vera Knee."

The camera pans to Charles and Vera. Charles looks at the lens—gravely, his eyes in a slight squint: his literary lion look. Vera—barely legal, Kabuki white skin, dark eyes, and storm clouds of black hair, wearing a halter top, a turquoise fucking halter top—giggles and waves disarmingly, jangling sixteen bracelets.

"Charles Davis hardly needs an introduction. His first book, *Life and Liberty*, made him an overnight literary sensation at the age of twenty-four. Universally considered the definitive novel about the Vietnam War, it has been translated into twenty-two languages and is taught in virtually every college in America. Mr. Davis has just published his sixth novel, *Capitol Offense*."

Derek holds up a copy of the 437-page book.

"Set in Washington's corridors of power, it focuses on a married senator who has an affair with an idealistic young congresswoman. Welcome to *Book Talk*, Charles."

"It's nice to be back, Derek."

"Also joining us is one of America's hottest young writers, Vera Knee. Vera's first novel, *Honey on the Moon*, a daring and hilarious look at life among Manhattan trendsetters, is delighting critics and readers alike."

Derek holds up *Honey on the Moon*, all 161 (small format) pages.

"Welcome to *Book Talk*, Vera."

"Hi."

She waves those damn jangling bracelets again.

"First of all, Charles, I want to tell you how much I enjoyed *Capitol Offense*. It's really about the abuse of power, isn't it? The senator's manipulation of the congresswoman is almost painful to read."

"Well, you know, Derek, power is the great aphrodisiac," Charles says. He rather likes these TV things. He tapes them secretly and watches them in the afternoon, a guilty pleasure.

"*Life and Liberty* has become a modern classic. Some critics have complained that your work since has grown increasingly commercial."

Charles smiles. "You'd never know it from my royalty statements."

"Have you felt a certain pressure in your subsequent works to live up to that early promise?"

Asshole. "Obviously that kind of early success is a mixed blessing. But I think each of my books stands on its own."

"Yes, but haven't they all been compared to *Life and Liberty*?"

"I thought I was here to talk about *Capitol Offense*."

"I just thought you might like to enlighten Ms. Knee on the pitfalls of overnight fame."

Charles looks at Vera Knee. She *is* pretty adorable.

"Sock away the dough," he says.

"I read *Life and Liberty* at Bennington. It's very powerful." She pouts her lips at him.

"And how are you handling the success of *Honey on the Moon?*" Derek, charmed, asks.

"Giddily. But it's hardly the kind of serious work Charles Davis is known for."

Derek leans forward, chuckling, all over this fifteen-minute flash like dirt on a dog. "Well, I must say, the literary world seems to be taking the book very seriously indeed."

Vera smiles. They're ignoring Charles.

"What does the literary world know, Derek? They've got their heads buried in books half the time."

Derek laughs. Vera giggles. Charles manages a lip twitch that he hopes will pass for a smile.

5

AS THE ELEVATOR glides silently to the top of 30 Rockefeller Plaza, Anne feels her anxiety level soar with a synchronous velocity. It's been a hellish day. She's taking *Home* on-line, and the madly creative Silicon Alley company she contracted to design the website is also madly undisciplined and four weeks behind schedule. Her Winter Warmth bedding is selling out and the mill can't manufacture any more; it's already turning out her Summer Breeze line. The result: hundreds of disappointed customers. Then she butted heads with her art director over the cover of the spring catalog. The capper—HG-TV postponed the taping after the office had spent the whole day on high alert and best behavior. Anne wonders if she's in over her head, running a $30-million-and-growing business without a day of training. Well, as long as nobody else wonders, she'll be okay. She rests her head against the elevator wall and closes her eyes for a moment. She puts a hand gently on her belly. How long can she keep it a secret? Now she has to face this party and make nice-nice with scores of friends, acquaintances, and ill-wishers. She flips open her compact and checks her lipstick. God, she looks pale. She gives her cheeks a quick pinch.

From atop the wide, fanned-out steps Anne surveys the crowd, the electric din, in the Rainbow Room. There is simply no place that distills the sheer heady excitement of Manhattan the way this glorious aerie atop Rockefeller Center does. The throng is just the right mix of publishing, society, celebrity, sprinkled with a touch of the art world, a dash of downtown, and the de rigueur drag queen or two. Glamour is like pornography, Anne thinks: I may not be able to define it but I sure know it when I see it. An enormous blowup of the jacket of *Capitol Offense* hangs from the ceiling, and a pyramid constructed of copies of the book sits on a round table in the center of the room. It's all flawless—perhaps she can salvage the day.

As Anne accepts and offers greetings, an arm shoots up from across the room. An elegant black arm encircled by three antique gold bracelets.

"Nina!" Anne says, crossing the room to give Charles's agent a strong hug. "Thank you for putting this together. It's perfect."

"Anything for our boy," Nina says. "You look fabulous, Anne. Of course."

"Look who's talking."

Nina Bradley wears her hair short, a cap of tight gray curls that sets off her sweeping jaw and long nose. Her dark eyes flash like obsidian; she's tall and moves like water. Tonight she's wearing a sleeveless black velvet top and black silk pants—one unbroken line of cool sophistication.

No one in New York gives Anne quite the same jolt of excitement that Nina does. The fact is that Anne with her Newport Beach pedigree—the Thatcher School, Stanford, swim team captain, country club superstar—Anne with the perfect legs, the perfect teeth, the perfect all-American ambition, idolizes black, savvy, self-made Nina Bradley.

Nina—somewhere in her sixties, in her very ripe prime, child of the Bronx, daughter of a subway motorman and a city clerk, both voracious readers who fed their daughter books—founded the country's second black-owned literary agency in 1955. For the first two years she lived on peanut butter, her only client a cartoonist syndicated in twelve black newspapers. But Nina was determined, she was smart, she was funny, and, yes, she was intensely beautiful.

Book by book, lunch by lunch, she built the Nina Bradley Agency into one of the country's top literary agencies, with a client roster that includes Pulitzer Prize and National Book Award winners. The writer who started the stampede, who really put her on the map, was a brilliant twenty-four-year-old, fresh out of Dartmouth, who'd written an electrifying novel based on his experiences as an army journalist during the Vietnam War. Charles sent Nina the book, having read a story about her in *Ebony*. They met for the first time, at his insistence, at a Ninth Avenue diner on a dark February evening twenty-five years ago. And ever since that day, she had presided over his career like a lioness.

"I hope Charles's taping went well," Anne says.

Nina reads Anne's anxiety and gives her hand a squeeze. "Charles is a pro."

Anne waves to an acquaintance and accepts a glass of Pellegrino from a passing waiter. "When do you think it'll show up on the best-seller list?"

"Within the month." Nina lowers her voice. "I hope."

"What do you mean, you *hope*?" Anne asks.

"Sales have been disappointing."

"How disappointing?"

Just as Nina is about to answer, a hush falls over the party. Anne and Nina turn. Charles is standing at the top of the entrance steps, leaning on the railing. They both know immediately: he's tight. The hairs on Anne's neck rise, and she shifts into damage-control. She sees a wave of sadness sweep over Nina's face.

The crowd breaks into applause. Charles smiles boyishly. "Aw, shucks," he says, all tousled hair and lopsided grin.

Anne is there quickly, ready. She gives him a kiss and leads him down the stairs, steering him through the throng with practiced grace. Her father once told her to learn from ducks on a pond: they glide across the surface seemingly without effort, but beneath the water line they're paddling like mad. Nina goes to meet them. She gives Charles a kiss on the cheek, and he smiles at her sheepishly.

"How did the interview go?" she asks.

"Derek Wollman was his usual boorish self, and my co-guest was the delightful Ms. Vera Knee, flavor-of-the-week. I barely got a word in between wisecracks." Charles reaches for a glass of champagne from a passing tray and downs it in one swallow. "Christ, I hate champagne," he says before grabbing another.

Nina puts a hand on Charles's forearm and applies pressure, keeping him from raising the glass to his lips.

"Charles, she's a flash in the pan. Your work will endure," Nina says, maintaining the pressure and looking him square in the eye.

"It will, darling," Anne adds.

"Well, I don't know if I can endure this party."

A well-dressed man who dwells somewhere on the periphery of the literary world—neither Anne nor Nina can remember his name—pushes into their circle.

"Charles, I can't wait to read this one," he says.

"Let me give you a piece of advice: don't bother."

"Excuse me?" the man says.

"I said don't bother. Read *Honey on the Moon* instead," Charles says, his voice rising. In concentric circles the room quiets.

"Darling . . ." Anne begins, but Charles is off.

"No, I'm serious, I think this charming fellow should skip my ponderous tome and escape into the giddy fucking joys of *Honey on the Moon*." By now you could hear a feather drop. "That's what they're lapping up at every airport and supermarket, cheap little feel-good books written in ten minutes by media-created hairdos with laptops who could retype the Brooklyn phone book, call it *Sugar on my Pussy*, and sell it for half a million dollars."

Nina leans into the nearest waiter and whispers, "Coffee. Fast."

Anne flashes a smile and says loudly, "Oh, Charles, stop quoting Shakespeare, this is a party."

The party gradually regains an uneasy equilibrium. Charles and Anne's allies pick up their conversations, a little too loudly. Many in the crowd are secretly thrilled by Charles's public meltdown, but etiquette demands they keep their claws sheathed, at least until the guest of honor leaves. Phones will be ringing all over Manhattan on this balmy fall night.

Nina plies Charles with coffee and hors d'oeuvres while Anne runs interference, both starting and finishing his sentences for him. As he sobers up and cools down, Charles, somewhat abashed but determined not to show it, accepts congratulations with a becoming modesty. Anne is livid with him, but more than that she's trying to interpret what Nina told her about the book's prospects. She has a pounding headache and knows she'll be sleeping with her tooth guard in. When things are more or less back on track, she excuses herself to go to the ladies' room. She dampens a paper towel and in the merciful quiet of a stall, holds it to her wrists and temples. Sitting there, she realizes how bad the timing of her pregnancy is. Morning sickness right up through the Christmas rush, dragging through the slush of February streets in maternity clothes, and then the baby coming in the spring—her busiest season, preparing the fall catalogs. But no, she admits, it isn't really the timing that's gnawing at her—she could schedule her way out of hell if she had to. It's the small flicker of doubt that flares up in the back of her mind, the possibility, however remote, that Charles isn't the father.

When she returns to the party, it's beginning to break up. For a moment, she can't find Charles in the emptying room. Then she sees him, slumped in a chair by a window, momentarily alone. Framed against the glittering skyline, he looks small, half-drunk and dazed. She goes to him.

6

LATE THAT NIGHT, deep in the fat, frightening marrow of the night, the demon hour, Charles lies in bed looking up at the ceiling. He's in an implosive rage—at that asshole Derek Wollman, at the asshole critics, at his asshole publisher, his asshole readers, the asshole world. He wrote a goddamn good book and they're all treating it like a piece of hack work. He's Charles Davis, for Christ's sake, he wrote one of the most important books of his generation. Do they really think people will be reading popcorn spy thrillers in a hundred years, crazy-girl memoirs, generational soap operas, trendy fluff tales? Of course they fucking won't be— they'll be reading Charles Davis.

As he lies coiled and obsessed, another emotion keeps trying to push up from beneath his rage. To keep it down he clings fiercely to his fury, because what lurks below it is unspeakable—the troll under the bridge, the mad twisted taunting troll: terror. Terror that he has lost it—his talent, his nerve, his edge—that the train has passed him by and he's the sad little man standing at the station growing smaller and smaller. Charles feels himself start to sweat.

He's from the most middle of middle-class backgrounds, both parents first generation off the farm and terrified of not fitting into their suburban Ohio world. His poor mother, Fran, lost without the ritual labor of farm life, was a stranger in a strange land, a walking nerve end, until the doctor put her on sedatives when Charles was about twelve, at which point she receded from her own life. Her expression grew perpetually startled, her eyes a little too wide open, startled at how frightening and incomprehensible life had turned out to be. Then there was Milton Davis, meek little Milton who lived and died by the rule book at Central Ohio Power and Light. The father who never took his son anywhere that the other middle managers weren't taking their sons—Little League games in the summer, the skating rink in the winter. Charles always thought of his parents as refugees trying desperately to fit into a foreign culture, a culture of blaring televisions and too much leisure and sleek appliances and cars that were like living rooms and living rooms that were never lived in.

And then Vietnam. The day after he graduated from high school, Charles enlisted, grabbing his ticket out of Fran and Milton's discreet suburban nightmare. Using his excellent grades in English, he snared a position on *Stars and Stripes*. It was basically a PR rag for the war effort, but there was no disguising the horror and deceit. As a journalist he had access not only to the troops but also to the men who were running the war, and in some ways their arrogance and indifference to human life were the most harrowing things of all. Vietnam exploded Charles's middle-class mind, made his parents' bourgeois terrors seem like an affront to the soul, an insult to the dead and dying. After the war, he went to Dartmouth on a scholarship and never looked back. By the time he graduated four years later, *Life and Liberty* was almost complete.

Milton and Fran are still living in that same box of a house, but now they spend the winter months in a stacked box on some bleak patch of Florida scrubland violated by dreary condo towers that look as if they belong in a working-class neighborhood of a Third World country. They visited New York a couple of times, but were overwhelmed by the city and ended up sequestered in their hotel room, phoning relatives back home, praising their son's generosity and keeping track of the weather and what was on sale at the supermarket.

Charles and his parents have whittled their communication down to three-minute Christmas and birthday phone calls in which they mouth numbingly rote sentiments. He has long since stopped seeking their approval. In truth, except for some ambiguous guilt after their phone calls, he feels virtually nothing toward them. Charles often wonders where his talent comes from, secretly believing that it's a greater gift for having sprung full blown from such barren soil.

Anne stirs beside him and he gets a gentle gust of her bath soap, crisp and citrusy. He hates her. He hates his parents. He even hates Nina, almost. Why hadn't she pushed him harder on *Capitol Offense*? She loved the idea originally. He can tell she isn't wild about the book; oh, she's steadfast and true, but he can tell. Charles's rage is making his temples throb. And then, like a bolt, he knows—knows what he has to do, where he has to go.

Charles gets out of bed and quietly slips into jeans and a T-shirt. He walks into the living room, picks up the phone, and calls his garage. "This is Charles Davis. I'll be picking up my car in ten minutes."

7

ANNE LIES STILL as Charles gets out of bed and leaves the room. The clock on her night table reads 4:36 A.M. Minutes pass and then she hears the front door close—no doubt he's off on one of his brooding nocturnal walks. Now she's alone in the apartment. Good. Yes, he's a great writer, yes, she has to make allowances, but that scene he threw at the Rainbow Room was infantile; they're going to be the laughingstock of Manhattan for the next month. She's fighting tooth and nail to hold her company together and he throws her a curve like that. Everything is always Charles! Anne tosses off the covers and walks down the long hallway into the living room. She opens the cabinet and clicks on the television, channel-surfing until she finds an infomercial for a line of skin-care products. The pitchwoman is a pretty young blonde who's got to be on speed; she's talking so fast she's almost slurring her words. Anne finds the mindless diversion comforting.

"All you pregnant women out there? Are you breaking out?

When I got pregnant with Amber, oh-my-God, I had the worst breakout of my life.''

Anne clicks off the television and lies down on the couch. She grabs a pillow and hugs it to her. The city is so quiet it's frightening. Try as she might to calm her mind, the memory keeps bubbling up like a toxic spring. . . .

It was the third week of August and New York was limping into its late summer wilt. Anne had just gotten off the plane from Savannah, the last leg of a southern buying trip in search of interesting folk art. Outside Savannah she had discovered a family living beside a tidal flat who made these extraordinary cloth dolls with handpainted eyes, whimsical and a little spooky. Perfect. But the rest of the trip had been a bust and Anne was exhausted when she climbed into the taxi at La Guardia. She rested her head on the back of the seat and closed her eyes as the driver made his way out of the airport.

Her cell phone rang. Anne debated whether or not to answer it and decided she had to.

"Yes?"

"Anne, it's John Farnsworth."

Farnsworth was the seventy-two-year-old financier and venture capitalist who had provided the start-up money for *Home*. He was from one of New England's oldest and wealthiest families; he and his wife, Marnie, longtime acquaintances of Anne's mother and stepfather, were high-profile philanthropists, pillars of Boston society.

"John, terrific to hear your voice. How are you?"

"Brutally hot up here in Cambridge."

"You're not in Maine?"

"Marnie's not well."

"I'm sorry to hear that."

"Listen, Anne, I just got off the phone with Ted Weiss."

Anne tensed. Ted was her chief financial officer. "I know, John, we lost money last quarter. But wasn't that projected?"

"It was. But not to this extent."

"Sales are incredible, it's costs that are killing us, but we're getting them down. I think it would be insane to compromise our standards; in the end they're what sets us apart."

"Anne, companies that don't make money can't stay in business."

"What are you saying?"

"I'm saying that I've got five million dollars invested in you, and now Ted Weiss tells me you need three million more. There comes a time when one has to cut one's losses."

"John, please, *Home* wasn't expected to turn a profit until next spring. We're a little behind where we want to be, but we're establishing a name for ourselves. So many exciting things are happening. Let me put together a presentation and I'll fly up tomorrow."

"Anne, you're a very talented and attractive woman and I'm always happy to see you, but I don't think this is going to work out."

Anne punched mute.

"Driver, turn around. Take me back to the airport."

It was Anne's first visit to Cambridge's Brattle Street neighborhood and she was dazzled. Enormous old mansions shaded by ancient trees lined the quiet streets, lawns stretched away to shaded dells, graceful fountains gurgled. There was a sense of order and security, of old wealth discreetly multiplying. Nothing evil would ever happen on these beautiful buffering streets.

On the plane Anne had spent twenty minutes meditating and then changed into a white linen shirt dress that hugged her derriere. She'd noticed John Farnsworth admiring her body on more than one occasion. She had the cabby stop at an antiquarian bookstore at the foot of Beacon Hill, where she bought a beautiful nineteenth-century edition of *Alice in Wonderland*. It set her back six hundred dollars, but she hoped it would turn out to be a wise investment. She knew the next hour could make or break her company, her dream.

The taxi turned into a circular driveway. The Farnsworth house was an immense stone Gothic surrounded by exquisite lawns and gardens. Anne got out of the cab. The air was heavy and fragrant. She closed her eyes, took two deep breaths, and rang the bell. The door was answered by a thin gray-haired woman in a uniform and crepe-sole shoes.

The front hall was the size of a small ballroom with dual parlors opening off it. Wood gleamed and glass sparkled; carpets cushioned and silk glistened. A Degas hung over a distant fireplace. The whole house was hushed as if in deference to the ailing Mrs. Farnsworth.

As the maid led her through a series of rooms, Anne thought: Do Americans still live like this? They came to a vaulted circular library with high stacks reached by a rolling staircase—a room that had awed Anne in *Architectural Digest*. The maid knocked gently on curved oak pocket doors.

"Yes?"

The maid slid one door open and then disappeared.

"Anne, come in."

John Farnsworth's inner sanctum was dominated by an enormous desk, a model schooner on a library table, and a painting of a black Labrador retriever over the mantel. The room smelled faintly of wood polish.

John sat behind the desk, his large head sporting a ring of white hair, jowls, and a ruddy spray of broken blood vessels. In a Wal-Mart he'd probably be taken for a retired pipe fitter who drank too much, but sitting there in his hunter-green blazer and tie, his flinty eyes flashing, his chin held at just the right angle, he oozed old-money confidence. He stood and shook Anne's hand.

"Welcome."

"The house is beautiful. I'm afraid *Home* can't compete." The last thing she'd want to compete with was this mausoleum.

"It's comfortable. Sit down."

Anne sat in an armchair and crossed her legs. The dress rode up her thighs.

"You look lovely, as always," he said.

"Thank you."

"How about a drink?"

"I would love a drink."

John crossed to the bar. "Name your pleasure."

"It's a long list."

"Why don't I open a bottle of Chardonnay?"

"That sounds perfect."

As John opened the wine, Anne looked around the room. The dog over the mantel was posed like a potentate, sitting up proudly, looking straight out. Like master, like dog. What would she do if he turned her down? Finding replacement financing would throw the company into full crisis mode, quality would suffer, and she'd have to let some people go.

John handed her a glass of wine and she took a sip. Superb. He sat back down.

"I brought you a little something," Anne said, handing him the book.

He opened it and looked at the illustrations for a moment.

"It's charming. Thank you." He put the book aside and looked Anne in the eye. "Weiss faxed me your numbers. The company could go either way."

That was Anne's cue to rock 'n' roll. She set her wineglass on the desk and leaned forward.

"The company is going only one way—up. People are talking about us. Our demographics are incredible: we're selling to the highest-income zip codes in the country. I've just set up an exclusive licensing agreement with a three-hundred-year-old Venetian glass company. We're going on-line; I'm talking to website designers tomorrow. We'll be able to sell globally, tailoring the catalog to each country's customs and tastes, and at the same time we'll save a fortune on paper and postage."

As he listened, Farnsworth drummed his fingers on a leather check ledger. "You're a very bright woman, Anne. I'm impressed. Always have been."

"Thank you. I'm very grateful for your support."

"You know what you want and you go for it. I used to be like that. Maybe I still am."

"That makes us kindred spirits."

"The market is sick with catalogs, Anne. I'd like to help you out, but I'm just not convinced."

Anne had come prepared to offer him another five percent of the company, but only as a last resort. She stood up and stretched back her shoulders, walked over to the window. At the far end of the lawn was a statue of a woman playing a harp. She turned and faced him. It was time to cut to the chase.

"What would it take to convince you?"

He considered her question, looking down at his hands. When he looked up he seemed distracted. "You're all business, aren't you, Anne?"

"I hope not." Had she played it wrong? Should she have taken a softer approach? She glanced at her watch; it was almost four o'clock. She hadn't eaten since early that morning, and the wine was making her light-headed and slightly dazed. The only thing she knew for sure was that she wasn't leaving that room without a commitment. "I just got back from a buying trip." She sighed. "It was 103 degrees in Savannah. Can you believe it?"

"Sounds hellish."

"This room is marvelously cool. These high ceilings." She carried her glass to a cracked leather sofa on the far side of the room and took a seat, crossing her legs again. "I fell in love with all this wood when I saw it in *Architectural Digest*. That painting's new," she said, indicating the dog.

"You don't miss a trick, do you, Anne?"

"I even sleep with my eyes open."

He laughed at this, in an admiring way. His teeth were beautiful—too beautiful; they couldn't possibly be original. She leaned forward on the couch and dropped her voice into an intimate register.

"John, this catalog is my baby. I will fight to the death to protect it. I will do *anything* to ensure its success."

He went to the bar, refilled his glass, and held up the bottle.

"Yes, please," she said.

In some strange way she was beginning to enjoy herself. Winning wasn't nearly as much fun without a few hurdles to jump over and she was certain she had just cleared a major one.

After refilling her glass he returned to his desk and took a pile of folders from a drawer. "Do you know what this is?" he asked, brandishing one.

Anne shook her head.

"It's a proposal I received three years ago from a young fellow out in Wisconsin who was producing those floppy stuffed animals my grandchildren can't get enough of. He wanted two million dollars. If I'd given it to him I'd have tripled my money by now. This is another proposal that came in at about the same time as yours. It's from a computer refurbishing company out in Palo Alto. They wanted three million. If I'd gone with them I would have cashed out for eight million. You don't get it, do you, Anne? You think you can waltz in here in that ass-hugging dress and dazzle me with pie in the sky and I'll just sit with my mouth open and cut you a check. *Home* is running twenty percent below projections, and you're starting to make me look like a fool. I'm a businessman, not a baby-sitter."

Anne felt as if she'd just been punched in the solar plexus. For one awful moment she missed her father. She looked down into her wineglass; her mouth tightened.

"*Home* is going to succeed," she said finally, firmly, trying to control her voice. She wasn't going to give him the satisfaction of an easy retreat. She looked up and met his stare. It was one of the hardest things she'd ever had to do.

He put the files back in the drawer and crossed to the couch, sat facing her at the other end, his arm draped across the back. There was a long silence. Anne heard the faint buzz of a lawn mower. "My wife is very ill," he said finally in a low voice.

Why was he telling her this? Now?

"I'm very sorry."

"We've made a sizable donation to the Museum of Fine Arts. They're naming a gallery in our honor. Marnie may not live to see the dedication ceremony."

It made Anne uncomfortable to have him so close. She should have waited until the next day, shown up bright and early with Trent in tow. This was all wrong.

"I'm not used to being alone," he said.

He lifted his hand and gently touched the back of her hair.

Anne took a measured sip of her wine, glancing at him over the rim of her glass. He looked nothing like the benevolent WASP grandfather who might sneak a glance at her thigh and nothing more.

"There's a superb restaurant that's opened a few blocks from here. I'd love to take you there for dinner. We can discuss the future, our partnership." He stroked her hair and then let his hand rest on her shoulder; it felt warm and heavy. "Some risks are worth taking, don't you think, Anne? I suppose that's what keeps life interesting. But I'm not in the mood to go over all the details at the moment. And you look a little tired yourself, my dear, all flushed and overheated. We can relax here for the rest of the afternoon. What do you say?"

Anne wanted to say "Fuck you and your money, you manipulative old lecher," but when she opened her mouth, "Sounds wonderful" came out.

"Shall I make the reservations for, say, seven o'clock, give you time to catch the last shuttle back to your famous husband?"

His hand was stroking her neck, trembling slightly with anticipation. His fingers slipped under her collar, dry and insistent.

"Seven o'clock is fine," she said.

He got up and walked to his desk and picked up the phone.
"Shall I draw the drapes?" he asked.

"Please," she said. "The sunlight is a little glaring."

Anne wakes with a start—what's she doing on the living room
couch? Early gray light pours in the windows, and for a moment
she's afraid. And then she remembers—the baby, the life growing
inside her. That goddamn unreliable diaphragm. She remembers
coming home from Cambridge, the money secured, but feeling
soiled, guilty, enraged. She will never give birth to Farnsworth's
child. But what if Charles is the father? Where is Charles? She sits
up and rubs her neck. He's not in the apartment; she can sense it.
He didn't come back last night. Anne feels that dreaded sense of
overload. She takes the whole mess and shoves it to one side of her
consciousness, out of view. Big day: she's going to crack the whip
on those website designers; she wants *Home* on-line in eight weeks
or they're history.

Tea, fruit, shower. Then it hits her—she knows where Charles
has disappeared to. Fine. She has her own problems. What she *will*
do is call the employment agency, hire that Emma, get Charles
moving whether he likes it or not. Anne gets up and heads into the
kitchen to start her day.

8

CHARLES SPEEDS ACROSS the George Washington Bridge
and onto the Palisades Parkway and then the New York State
Thruway, heading north, due north, away from the city. As the
first gray of morning spreads up from the eastern horizon, he
drives—the speedometer on his black Jaguar hovering around
80—through the lush, mottled Indian-summer landscape of the
Hudson Valley. From the car phone, he leaves Anne a message that
he has to get away. He speeds past Albany and still he drives north.
The ancient Adirondack Mountains, vast and virtually unpopulated,
loom up and encircle the Thruway with their deep green forests.
Charles feels he's entering uncharted terrain, a place where all
measures of ourselves must be recalibrated, where the forests and
lakes and mountains demand an honesty that matches their own.

Charles exits the Thruway and heads west, through tiny rustic
towns that survive on the trade of transient hunters and hikers.
Surrounded by the glorious riot of autumn, he drives for hours,
rarely seeing another car, deep into the wilderness, winding along

roads that tunnel through the endless forest. Finally he turns off paved road and onto a rutted, rocky track that jackknifes its way up a mountainside. He comes to a clearing that opens like a welcoming hand. There, perched on a rocky promontory above a small lake, sits a cottage that is the stuff of a hermit's dreams—weathered, snug, crisscrossed by an orgy of incestuous vines. Charles gets out of his car and savors the sight. The afternoon sun is warm on his face. He listens to the dueling calls of the mountain songbirds, takes a deep breath and tastes the cool air. He knows he's done the right thing, come to the right place.

"Take *that*, you little fuckers!"

Charles smiles at the sound of the familiar voice and walks around the side of the cottage. Making her way around the periphery of her garden with the aid of a cane, sprinkling deer poison as she goes, is Portia Damron—tiny Portia, well into her eighties, a Pall Mall sticking from her scowling lips, her weathered, wrinkled face a map of the world's sorrows.

"Hello, Portia."

Focused on her mission, Portia ignores his greeting, doesn't even glance in his direction. "There's only one thing in this world I hate more than people—deer. *Bambi* was a pack of lies. They should make a sequel and reveal them for what they are: pesky, voracious, and disease-carrying." She angrily jiggles her cane in the direction of a half-devoured cabbage.

The job done, Portia straightens up and meets Charles's eyes for the first time. "You look like hell, Charles. Of course, you live in hell, so it's no wonder." Without waiting for a response, she heads toward the cottage. "Sun's just about past the yardarm. Let's have a martini and try to forget we're alive."

As a chicken roasts in the enormous old cast-iron oven, Charles sits by the fire with his feet up. He feels utterly at home, safe and protected in the cavelike cottage with its overflowing ashtrays and half-filled coffee cups and books, books everywhere—overflowing the shelves that line the walls, heaped in piles on the floor, spilling off tables and chairs. Across the room in the open kitchen Portia is whipping up dinner—between drags on her Pall Mall—with a vigor that belies her years. Root vegetables, tiny red potatoes, a salad of the season's last greens, corn bread—suddenly Charles is ravenous.

"That smells fantastic."

"It's all fresh. Primitive. Nothing like it."

"God, it's good to be up here."

"And to what do I owe?"

"I just needed to kick back and relax."

"My bullshit alarm just went off." Portia looks up from the sink where she's washing the greens and eyes Charles with piercing honesty. "Except for a perfunctory phone call now and then and an Anne Turner Christmas card that managed to be hideously sentimental and depressingly trendy at the same time, I've barely heard from you in the past year. Now you show up without notice and want me to believe you're here to kick back and relax?"

Charles knows she has him, of course; he has traveled up here to be had. It's time to get honest with the one person who knows him better than any other. He stands and begins to pace around the room.

"You know what I admire about you, Portia?"

"I hope more things than we have time to discuss."

"You were a legend. You could have taught forever. But when you felt your time was up, you quit."

"When I had nothing more to say, I quit," Portia answers, drying the greens on a soft old dish towel.

"Exactly. You quit. With dignity and grace."

"And a damn good pension. What's your point?"

"Have you read the new Mailer?" Charles asks.

"It's brilliant. Too long, but brilliant."

"And the new Styron?"

"Short, but also brilliant."

Charles stops his pacing and looks out the window at the lake below. It's just past twilight—that sweet fleeting in-between time—and the lake glows like an indigo jewel. "And my latest?"

Portia stops what she's doing and considers for a moment. "Exactly the right length."

Charles sits back down and instead of denying his hurt allows himself to accept it. "I wondered why I hadn't heard from you."

"I thought I'd wait until I was asked."

In the silence that follows, Portia begins tossing the salad. "Do you remember your story about the Vietnamese whore nursing her baby?"

"That was the first story I ever wrote," Charles says, remembering that dusty Saigon street corner, the painted whore just past puberty, the suckling infant, the nineteen-year-old boy, Charles, who watched them, fascinated, before finally approaching the mother, the child-mother, and offering her candy and money, which she accepted greedily, with a suggestive leer, her baby still hanging off her nipple.

"When you stood up in class and read it, I started to sweat with excitement."

Charles looks into the fire. "But what if there is no more? What if I have nothing left to say?"

"If I believed that, I wouldn't be wasting my time listening to you." Portia takes the chicken out of the oven. It's a succulent golden brown, surrounded by roasted potatoes, turnips, carrots, and onions. "Let's eat. We have a lot of talking to do."

Later, deep in the deep Adirondack night, Portia sits in her favorite chair while Charles paces. The picked-over dinner and empty wine bottles cover the table, the air is thick with smoke from Portia's endless stream of Pall Malls, and the fire is a rubble of glowing red embers. Charles is in that realm beyond fatigue, where the mind finds its third wind and a terrible clarity takes hold.

"What's that line at the end of *Gatsby,* when Nick talks about leaving the East? 'So when the blue smoke of leaves . . .' " Charles says, shutting his eyes as he searches for the words.

Portia is right there: " 'When the blue smoke of brittle leaves was in the air and the wind blew the laundry stiff on the line—' "

" 'I decided to come back home.' That's it. That's the kind of simple, clear poetry I want," Charles says. "Nothing extra, every word exact. Not one comma out of place: 'The blue smoke of brittle leaves . . .' "

Fitzgerald's words hang in the air. Charles sinks into a chair and feels the last years—the fearsome task of dredging up yet another book, the tightening vise of expectation, the bitter disappointment, the seductive call of cynicism—coming home to roost on his tired bones. He's at ground zero, defenseless.

"I've lost it, Portia. My inspiration. My will. The kid who wrote that story is dead."

The weight of their history, their love, bears down on Charles. Portia is the closest thing to a parent, a real parent, that he has ever had. He can feel something like tears coming up inside him. He fights down the queasy feeling in his chest, the burning behind his eyes. He wants to turn and look at her, but doesn't think he could hold her gaze. He lets his head roll back on the chair and closes his eyes.

From across the room, Portia studies him carefully.

Out in the moonless night the water, the forest, and the sky are endless and implacable. Portia's living room window casts a soft yellow glow into the vastness.

How different the world looks in the morning. What seemed like hell the night before turns out to be merely purgatory, as if the dark's demons are unable to survive the infusion of light. Portia is up and about long before Charles wakes from a profound sleep, feeling rested for the first time in recent memory. For a long time he lies on the narrow single bed in Portia's cluttered spare room, listening to the dense quiet of the woods.

Something happened the night before: his logjam broke, and he can feel the cooling waters of hope flow through him. Maybe it was just admitting—to Portia, yes, but more important, to himself—how scared he is. He has begun to take measure of himself; just coming up here has been a first step.

After a quiet breakfast of blueberry corncakes, eggs laid ten minutes earlier and fried crisp around the edges, and strong coffee spiked with chicory, Portia and Charles head outside, out to the lake, to fish. And to talk. They make their way slowly down the rickety wooden steps that lead down the steep, rocky cliff to the water. The deserted lake is glorious in the morning sun. They climb into Portia's battered rowboat, and she takes the oars while Charles readies the fishing rods.

"The little shits are down there laughing at us," Portia says as they head out to the middle of the lake.

"Let's hope they're laughing with their mouths open."

Portia pulls up the oars and takes her rod from Charles. They both cast off, breaking the still water with soft splashes. They fish in silence, a sympathetic calm settling over them.

"Portia, I need to make a lot of money. I'm in over my head," Charles says finally.

"Write as if you have a hundred million in the bank," Portia says dismissively.

"It's awfully easy for you to say that, up here with nothing to lose."

"I have *you* to lose, Charles, and I don't want to. . . . Or have I already?"

"What's that supposed to mean?"

"Was coming up here just a little game to play with yourself, a cut-rate therapy session, a way to prove you really are an artist, to pay your psychic dues? Because if it was, I have better things to do with my time."

Charles closes his eyes for a moment, examining his own motives. His actions in the months ahead will determine what kind of man he really is. He needs to prove himself again, to Portia, to Anne, to Nina—and to himself.

"You know how important you are to me, Portia. You know how much of *Life and Liberty* is yours. Remember those glorious, grueling months up in Hanover? You took the raw material and molded it into that book."

"I did. But you wrote it."

"I need your help again. I'm lost. I have no idea what to write about."

A blue heron, majestic and prehistoric, rises up from the shore and flies away over the treetops. Portia shades her eyes to watch its ascent. She keeps her eyes on the sky long after the bird is out of sight.

"Sometimes inspiration comes to us. Sometimes we have to go searching for it," she says.

"Where?"

"Only you can answer that question. There's a lot at stake here, Charles. Of course I'll help you. But you've got to be willing to work, to break out of that velvet-lined rut you're in."

And then Portia gets a bite. Bracing herself, she deftly reels in her line until a large, thrashing trout breaks the water. She grabs the fish with one hand, the hook gleaming as it pierces the scaly flesh, the animal's body whipping wildly in her grasp.

"Look at this fish, Charles. It's fighting, it's fighting for its life." In a swift, practiced move she pulls out the hook and holds up the struggling fish. "As long as we breathe, that's what we have to do. We have to fight. We have no choice. There's a price tag on every gift."

Portia tosses the fish back into the water. Spared, it plunges down to the depths, shimmery and alive.

"Now get back down to that city and get to work."

9

CHARLES TOSSES HIS BAG on a bench in the foyer and walks through the kitchen and down the long hallway that leads to his two-room office. He's brought up short by the sight of a young woman sitting at the desk in the outer office. Plain as toast, she's wearing a gray flannel skirt, a cream blouse, and a navy sweater-vest. Her wavy brown hair is pulled back with a small band and she has on no makeup at all, as far as Charles can tell. She looks up from a copy of *Bleak House*, startled by his abrupt arrival. She stands quickly, flustered and awkward, smoothing out her skirt.

"That's the one Dickens I've never read," Charles says.

"I have this stupid rule about finishing every book I start," the young woman says.

"I suppose that's honorable. Let me guess—you're that whiz of a temp who's going to whip my office into shape and turn my life around."

A furious blush flies up the girl's pale neck and Charles feels a familiar surge of power. She's so harmless, so hopeless, no doubt incredibly efficient. And she has a certain clumsy charm. It's so like Anne to do this without getting his okay. For a moment, Charles considers sending the girl home.

"Your wife called my agency. She told me to wait for you to get home, that you'd arrive sometime this afternoon."

Charles glances around him. The room is strewn with tottering piles of unanswered mail, unfiled contracts, unread manuscripts, newspapers and magazines filled with articles he's never gotten around to clipping. "Well, as a matter of fact, I do want to get this mess organized," he says.

"I think I could be of some help with that."

"Would you like to see the rest of the operation?" he asks.

The young woman nods and Charles unlocks his inner office. He's proud of this room, even in its current disheveled condition. There are the framed posters of his book jackets; the photographs of Charles with everyone from Jack Nicholson, who starred in the movie of *Life and Liberty*, to François Mitterrand, who made him a member of the French Legion of Honor; the Eames bookshelves filled with foreign-language editions of his work; the Frank Lloyd Wright desk. Two windows look out over the treetops of Central Park.

"What a beautiful place to write," the young woman says with undisguised awe.

"I wrote my first book in a freezing trailer outside of Hanover, New Hampshire."

"*Life and Liberty?*"

"Yes."

"I loved that book."

"It must have seemed like ancient history to you."

"No," she says, suddenly very serious and resolute. "It seemed timeless." And then, as if taken aback by the confidence in her own voice, she looks down, running a fingertip over her thumbnail, frowning. When she looks up she manages a wan, haunted smile. "I should start on the outer office. I don't want to disturb you."

Charles studies her a moment before answering. "I'm not a shrinking violet. If you're disturbing me, I'll let you know. Basically, I work from seven to four. Aside from that, I like my coffee black, when I smoke I smoke Marlboros, when I drink I drink Chivas, and when I'm on a roll I crave hot dogs and stacks of french fries slathered with mayonnaise. Come on, I'll show you the filing system. Oh, by the way, I didn't get your name."

The young woman looks at Charles and he's taken aback by her arresting eyes. Up close, he can see that they're an iridescent green, lightly flecked with brown. They meet his gaze and hold it.

"It's Emma. Emma Bowles."

10

CHARLES STANDS BY the bar in the living room mixing himself a Scotch and water and looking out at the autumn glory of Central Park. There's something about the girl, Emma, that intrigues him. Those eyes. The nervous habit she has of rubbing her thumbnails with her fingertips. He finds her touching. It'll be nice having her around for a while.

The front door opens and Anne glides in, breathless, wearing a green suit with navy trim. She goes to Charles and gives him a kiss, avoids looking him in the eye.

"Welcome home, stranger," she says.

"It's good to be back."

"Am I interrupting something?"

"Of course not. Drink?"

"Yes, please—ginger ale."

"You look terrific," he says. She doesn't really; she looks tense and there are dark circles under her eyes.

"I got a trim today. A first: Marcus came into the office to do it. I felt so decadent, like Nancy Reagan. Or Madonna.'' She slips off her shoes and tucks her feet under her as she sinks down on one of the two enormous white sofas that face each other in front of the fireplace. ''Next I'll be putting in a little private gym, or maybe a whole mini-spa, with one of those tiny pools that churn a current against you.''

Anne's got the charm machine cranked up to overdrive—one of her diversionary tactics. She still hasn't looked him in the eye. No doubt she's angry at him for leaving in the middle of the night, angry and also waiting for him to mention the girl, Emma, to thank her for hiring her. There's a silence as each waits for the other to make the next move. Charles yields.

''Thank you for hiring that secretary. I think you're right, it will be easier with things sorted out in there.''

''You're welcome,'' Anne says simply, smart enough not to milk her small triumph. ''She's really quite bright and efficient.''

''She seems to be.''

''She certainly didn't get where she is on her charm. Although she does have a certain wounded-fawn je ne sais quoi. In any case, I'm glad you think she'll work out.''

''I do. She's unobtrusive.''

''I must say though, Charles, I wish you'd woken me. I worry when you disappear like that.''

His work is one issue that isn't open to compromise. ''I had to go. I went.''

''And how's the great lady?'' Portia brings out Anne's insecurity. She's convinced his mentor dismisses her as shallow and unworthy, feels Charles would have been better off marrying some bookish trust-fund baby who lived only to nurture his fiery muse, who would create a cozy cocoon in some posh Vermont hollow, complete with a rustic studio out back and two apple-cheeked children.

Charles sits on the arm of the opposite sofa and runs a fingertip along the rim of his glass. ''She's herself.''

''And did she give you what you needed?''

Charles resents that question, as if something as complex and painful and important as his work can be reduced to a yes or no. He crosses to the window. The October dark has arrived and the lights have come on in Central Park. The cars zipping through the park look like mad Tinkertoys. Finally he turns and looks at Anne. There's genuine concern in her face. "It was a good trip."

"I'm glad, darling. Phoebe adored *Capitol Offense*, was up all night reading it, now everyone in the office is clamoring for a copy. I said, 'Absolutely not—go out and buy it.' "

Charles sits next to her on the sofa. She reaches out and strokes his cheek. He takes her hand and kisses it. "Next time I go I'll leave a note."

"Make it a love note."

He places her hand on his thigh and runs his fingertips between her fingers. He's been boorish and self-obsessed lately—it's time to give Anne something she wants.

"Anne?"

"Yes?"

"About a baby? There'll always be a thousand reasons to wait."

She turns away abruptly, withdrawing her hand. She really does look exhausted.

"I didn't get a great deal of sleep last night. Can we discuss this some other time? Right now I need a nap. You know we have to be at Lincoln Center at eight."

"I'm not going." She freezes. "I'm sorry, Anne, I've made a decision to cut back on my socializing. It's for my work."

"Nice of you to tell me."

"I really have to focus. It's important."

"I understand that, darling, but I think I have a right to be informed of these decisions, maybe even consulted. This is for the Fresh Air Fund, Charles, they do important work. And the tickets were five hundred dollars."

Low blow. "If you can't afford them you shouldn't have bought them."

Anne concedes the point with an almost imperceptible nod.

She finishes her drink with a long swallow. "Am I supposed to just cancel our entire calendar, or should I find myself a walker? Too bad Jerry Zipkin is dead."

"There's that artist—what's his name? You love his company."

"I can't believe this. You're my husband, Charles."

"I also happen to be a novelist."

"Are the two mutually exclusive?"

"They may be for a little while."

Anne stands up. Something hardens in her face, around the mouth. "Keep me posted," she says, and walks out of the room.

Charles watches her go. The apartment feels polluted by their exchange. Why the hell did she bring up a piddling five hundred dollars like that, with the money she makes? She has every right to be angry about his backing out of the benefit, but it won't last. She'll go by herself, make some excuse for his absence, and have a terrific time. Anne's a big girl, and she'll soon see that he's doing this for both of them. If he can come up with fifty really strong pages, Nina will snare a serious advance and everyone will breathe easier. But fifty pages of what? Does Portia think that some idea is just going to crash through the window and—*pow!*—he'll have another great book? She sure as hell doesn't have much respect for his process. That's unfair. She's *part* of his process. At least she used to be.

Charles grabs the bottle of Scotch off the liquor tray and heads for his office.

11

EMMA SITS AT her desk sorting through months of old mail. Many of Charles's fans, particularly the female ones, seem to project their deepest longings—for a son, a husband, a lover—onto him. In her week and a half on the job, she's dealt with a pound cake sent by a sixty-two-year-old widow in Missouri, a naked photo from a married woman in Marina Del Rey, and an impenetrable love poem from an overwrought Wellesley freshman. And then there are the manuscripts sent in by would-be writers, and galleys sent by publishers hoping to garner a book jacket blurb. When she started, there were dozens of these lying around the office. She suggested to Charles that she read the books and write synopses for him to review. He praised her initiative, and using this system they're working their way through the backlog. Ditto for the forty-two unreturned phone calls that greeted her on her first day.

Emma has a goal: to make herself indispensable to Charles Davis.

The mail sorted into its usual three piles—Throw Out, Answer, and Pass On—Emma looks up and surveys the office. There's no doubt that she's succeeded in bringing some semblance of order to the chaos. There are neat piles of papers on chairs and tabletops, each pile labeled with a Post-it note as to its eventual destination. The room is off-limits to the housekeeper and Emma spent her first days cleaning, stirring up volumes of dust that sent her into sneezing fits. But what a difference—the place shines. There's even a vase of fresh flowers on her desk. Emma loves order—it calms her, quells her terrors.

Emma imagines Charles, on the other side of the closed door between the two offices, sitting at his desk, writing. He has told her he's starting a new book, that he writes his first drafts in longhand in spiral notebooks he orders from the Dartmouth bookstore. She's read all of his novels. Her favorite is *Irreparable Damage*, the story of a New England family coming apart after the sudden death of the mother. The father, a college professor, mad with grief, immediately begins an affair with one of his students. Emma understood completely the professor's need to lose himself in passion even though he knew that the affair was wrong and would damage his children, the young woman, and himself. Emma had been moved by the book and found solace in it too. There was something about that family, floundering in the aftershock of sudden tragedy, that made her feel less alone.

And of course she's fascinated by the man himself. Beneath his imposing manner he seems kind, even wounded, lonely somehow, like a little boy who has won first prize at the fair but now stands all alone behind the bandstand. She wonders if he has any friends, any real friends. He needs one. She loves his hands, the long fingers with squared tips. When he gets close to her she can smell his pine soap.

As for Anne Turner, Emma hates her. She'd like to take a hammer to those perfect teeth. The bitch knows exactly what she wants, is so damned articulate that words roll off her tongue as if they were scripted. Turner lives in a parallel universe where every-one is fearless and graceful, where life is just a matter of waking up and making fabulous things happen. Emma keeps her mouth shut during their brief encounters. She listens attentively and tries to look intelligent, always remembering a secret maxim she honed in the mental hospital: What you don't say can't be used against you. During her week temping at *Home*, Emma had observed Anne carefully, hoping to learn some of her tricks. Even that rainy day in her office, when Anne got that phone call that seemed to disturb her so much, she never lost her composure. She was told some-thing, some piece of news—what could it have been?—and her face went white. She even forgot Emma was in the room.

Turner had told Emma to help herself to anything in the kitchen, and two days ago, when Charles Davis was at the other end of the apartment taking a shower, she had walked down the long hallway and into the enormous room. She'd opened the re-frigerator door and looked at all the cheeses and chutneys and tiny pickled vegetables. Each label was a miniature work of art; all the food seemed to come from organic farms in quaint-sounding cor-ners of Connecticut or the Hudson River valley. Emma opened a small container of goat cheese—it smelled like goat hair. Stupid fucking rich people. She spit into it. Then, giggling to herself, she stirred the spit with her pinky until the saliva disappeared. She imagined Anne Turner spreading the cheese on a cracker and re-marking on how divine it was. Then Emma took a carrot from the crisper. She'd taken only one bite when she heard Charles Davis approaching. She dashed back down to the office and stuffed the uneaten carrot into her purse. She smiled at him when he came in.

Charles's office has antique filing cabinets, a Persian rug, and twelve-foot ceilings. Emma feels as if she's stepped through the looking glass into a world she's read about and seen on television. And now she's part of it.

No you're not. Stupid Emma, you're a fly to these people, a convenience. You don't belong here. Freak! Go back to where you came from, hide away in some rented room, be a small-town weirdo. Emma clenches her fists, digs her fingernails into her palms, harder harder. . . .

There's a tentative knock on the door at the end of the hallway. Emma licks a sliver-moon of blood from her palm. Be calm be cool. She goes and opens the door. Magdalena, the housekeeper, a quiet woman from the Canary Islands who pretends she doesn't speak English—Emma sees through *her* little act—is standing there with a FedEx letter in her hand.

As Emma walks back down the hallway, she looks at the return address and sees that the letter is from London, from Charles Davis's British publisher. She stands still and listens and then knocks lightly. Silence. Then the door flies open.

"What do you want?" Charles Davis demands. His face looks pained, almost contorted.

"This Federal Express letter just arrived from your British publisher. I thought it might be important."

"You *thought* it might be important?"

"Yes."

Charles grabs the letter, tears it in two, and flings it in the trash. "I'm trying to write! I don't care if Jesus Christ himself wants to meet me for lunch, I'm not available to the world until further notice. Is that so goddamn hard to understand?" After shooting her a look of pure condescension, he slams the door in her face.

Emma stands there, a sickening deadweight suddenly lodged in her stomach. The sensation begins as a purely physical one, but quickly moves up her body, until her mind implodes with dismay, dismay and an approaching panic. She feels herself start to sweat on her upper lip, her forehead, under her arms. She feels the first tingle of prickly heat. She knows what comes next—banishment. Out to the back landing at the top of the stairs in her thin cotton dress and her bare feet, the door slamming and then locking behind her, the hours passing, she forbidden to move, staring at the railing, at the grooves in the wood, dreading that she'll be noticed by the family that lives across the way. There are six kids in the family—six rowdy, unwashed, laughing, loved kids—and when they see Emma they stare, too kind to laugh. Then they whisper and run away, as if her sorrow might be catching. And evening turns to night and Emma grows colder and wants to cry, but what's the use? And the hunger grows so intense it finally disappears and at least when it's dark no one can see her up there on the back landing at the top of the stairs at the end of the alley in her bare feet and thin cotton dress with nothing on underneath.

Emma stands in front of the door to Charles's office. What should she do? *Don't panic.* She stands stock-still, her breathing shallow. She clenches her fists and wills herself not to cry. She hears what sounds like Charles Davis falling to the floor, followed by loud breathing, as if he's doing a series of push-ups. This is followed by pacing. Then silence.

"Emma?"

"Yes, Mr. Davis?" she answers through the closed door.

"For Christ's sake, stop calling me Mr. Davis. And will you please come in here?"

Emma opens the door and takes a step into the inner office. He's sitting at his desk. "It's Charles."

Emma hesitates a moment before saying a soft "Charles."

"That's better." He smiles. "Sit down." Emma sits across from him in a wooden armchair. "When I'm writing, or trying to write . . . well, it's a difficult process, agonizing, fucking hellish is what it is. I don't understand it. It's physical, like football, or combat even, only the enemy is some amorphous gorilla of the soul. Or some bullshit like that. Is this making any sense?"

"Yes."

"I suppose my point is, I become keyed up, revved, I go a little crazy. Or a lot crazy. So if I scream and yell and pound the walls . . . well, it's not you."

Emma feels a surge of gratitude and reaches past it to grasp courage. "I know that," she says.

"You do?"

". . . Charles . . . I've read all your novels. I've read *Irreparable Damage* twice. I can't even imagine what it must take to create like that."

Charles doesn't answer, but a little smile plays at the corners of his mouth.

"I'm not afraid of a little screaming and yelling," Emma says.

"No?"

"Not if that's what it takes."

He leans toward her, across his desk. "I'm very glad to hear that, Emma."

"Scream away," she says with a smile of her own.

He nods. Emma stands up to go.

"And, Emma?" She turns and looks at him, into his eyes. "You're doing a very good job."

She nods and closes the door quietly behind her. When she settles into her desk she tries to get back to work, but can't. She's overwhelmed by a physical sensation that moves over her body like liquid, a warm want that she has never felt before. There's no way this job will be over in six weeks—she'll make sure of that.

12

"This is it," the bored, harried young man in the inexpensive gray suit says with undisguised distaste, before lighting a Salem to recover from the four-story climb.

Emma takes one look at the semifurnished studio and says, "I'll take it."

She takes out her checkbook—her first ever checkbook—and slowly writes out a check for the first and last month's rent plus the $200 key deposit the managing agent insists on.

The agent—who Emma notices has a smudge of hair dye on one ear—examines the check and slips it into his pocket. He hands her the keys, mumbles a cynical "Enjoy," and leaves without closing the door behind him. Emma watches him go down the stairs. There's a ball of greasy paper on the second-to-last step. She hopes he slips and breaks his neck.

Emma loves the sound the old lock makes when she turns it and the bolt slides into the wall. Then she turns and surveys the first home that she can call her own.

The apartment is just one long room with three windows along one wall and a kitchen built into the far end. It smells faintly of soy sauce and fried dumplings, courtesy of the Chinese restaurant on the ground floor. The walls are the color of tobacco spit. There's a double bed, a laminate desk, an ornate white dresser making a sad stab at French Regency, its top notched with cigarette burns, a frameless mirror above the dresser. Emma loves the cigarette burns; she runs her finger over the blackened hollows and imagines a poet, a bad girl, a good cop, a lost junkie from the Midwest who was once somebody's son—all the Manhattan stories this room has hosted. Or maybe just one sad fat old woman lived here for twenty years eating junk food and smoking Winstons until her heart gave out.

The Chinese restaurant has a red neon sign that snakes up the building and suffuses the room with a rosy glow, even in the afternoon light. Emma looks down at the street and sees an old Italian woman in widow's blacks walking a just-groomed white poodle. She loves this shabby patch of the city where Chinatown, Little Italy, and the Lower East Side converge.

Continuing her inspection, Emma pushes open the door to the bathroom. She stops—the bathtub *that* bathtub.

"Time for your bath, Emma." They both knew what those words meant, the cheerful singsong a cruel mockery of their true intent. Emma would scuttle under her bed, stare up at the rusty springs, her head throbbing with dread and fear. "Didn't you hear me, honeybunch? I said it's time for your splish-splash." And then the high-heeled mules would appear in the doorway and approach the bed and Emma would scoot farther under, as far away as she could get. "Where's my little Mouseketeer? We have got to get you clean if we want Daddy to come home. You want Daddy to come home, don't you?" And then her mother's skinny arm with its gaggle of Bakelite bracelets would reach down under the bed, the hand grabbing at the air like a blind woman's, grasping the first

thing it touched—an arm, a leg, a hank of hair—and pull Emma
out across the slippery linoleum floor. "Oh, Emma, if you don't
watch out, that expression will freeze on your face forever. I'll
have to put you in a zoo with the other monkeys. Daddy won't
want a dirty monkey around the house." And then that laugh, that
throaty staccato laugh. "Come on, monkey." She'd lift her up—
Emma going as rigid as a stick—and carry her into the bathroom,
set her down. "Can't take a bath in a dirty little dress, said the owl
to the pussycat." She'd stand there watching Emma under the light
of that burning naked bulb that dangled from the ceiling like a
hanged man. Then she'd bang down the toilet seat and sit down
casual as day, crossing her long legs, humming brightly, checking
out her painted nails. Emma would hug herself and look down—
then suddenly the slap would smash across her cheek and she'd
swear she would die before her mother saw her tears. "Silly fiddle-
faddle! I got all night to party." Slowly, slowly, Emma would lift
the thin dress over her head—the thin blue flannel dress that
smelled like her sheets, her nubby bed-wetted sheets. "Splish-
splash, I was taking a bath, all on a Saturday night." Emma would
look over at that tub, that big old clawfoot tub with the chipped
porcelain finish. It looked as big as a house. Filled with two inches
of the coldest water that pipes could produce. "Daddy's gonna
come back, Emma baby, and we're all gonna move to a fishing
shack on the Gulf Coast, lie in the sun and smoke reefer and paint.
Now you gonna get in that water or not, you little piece of shit?"
And Emma would step into the tub. At least in the tub she could
huddle over, hug herself, hide her body from her mother's eyes.
The water was so cold it hurt and she'd close her eyes and clench
her teeth and wait for what she knew was coming. It'd start on her
lower back—the loofah mitt, the frayed loofah mitt from Wal-
green's. At first her mother used a light touch and Emma always
had a moment of sweet hope that it would be different this time.
"How do you get so dirty, you cute little nasty thing? Your father
knew you were a dirty girl, didn't he? That's why he ran away, to
get away from you, you dirty thing." And as she talked, she'd

press harder with the mitt, scrubbing Emma's back and then her shoulders and then pushing her back in the tub and scrubbing her chest and stomach and her thighs, pushing her legs open and scrubbing until little red pinpricks covered Emma's body. "Filthy little girl, dirty dirty Emma. Daddy hates dirty girls. I'm going to make you clean. Clean clean clean. Scrubba-dub-dub, two freaks in a tub." And that naked blinding bulb swung overhead. And finally, when her whole body burned and went numb, Emma would float up from the bathtub and look down at her mother scrubbing away, sometimes sprinkling Comet on the loofah mitt—she'd watch as the little girl's skin got redder and redder, watch as the weird woman did mean things to the little girl. Mean mean things.

Emma stands in the bathroom doorway taking deep breaths. She makes herself look at the rest of the room. The floor is black-and-white linoleum tile. There's a pedestal sink with a medicine chest above it. Emma resolutely pushes down her pants and sits on the toilet, leaving the door open. As she pees, she slowly forces her eyes over to the tub. It's just a bathtub. Her bathtub. But she doesn't deserve a bathtub—she's a dirty girl. Emma feels the dread spreading like a stain, the familiar tightening in her throat, the queasiness in her stomach; her jaw goes slack and her eyes half close. Moving slowly, she stands up from the toilet, slips off her pants, takes the little tin box from her bag, and climbs into the tub. She crouches down with her legs spread. She runs her fingers over the tiny raised scars that line her inner thigh. The scars are her friends. But no more scars. She's learned that. Don't press too hard and you won't leave a scar. So she opens the box, lifts the velvet, takes the razor and presses gently against her skin—just hard enough for the sweet obliterating pain to bring up a perfect line of blood.

13

ENTHRALLED, ANNE DRAGS the sumptuous virtual sofa down from the corner of the computer screen and moves it around the tiny virtual room until she finds just the spot for it. She resumes browsing through *Home On-line*, dragging down one item after another until the room is, well, perfect. Then she orders the items she wants by moving around the room and clicking on them. That's all it takes. The warehouse outside Poughkeepsie ships the products; credit card billing is instantaneous.

"Absolutely fabulous," Anne says, turning to a beaming Nikki Spinoza, the genius behind InterMagic, a woman in her early forties who wears her extra poundage sans apology, dresses in thrift-store rejects, lets her flyaway hair fly away, makes no secret of her lesbianism, and runs a very loose ship. InterMagic is housed in a converted stable in Tribeca. The staff, none of whom looks over twenty-five, are encouraged to bring in their latest toys, and the yeasty chaos—strewn with everything from a beach ball to a four-foot robot—resembles a kindergarten classroom.

"I'm glad you like it," Nikki says.

"Nobody else in the industry has anything approaching this. It's more like playing a game than shopping. How soon can we have the site up and running?" Anne asks.

"A week."

Anne feels that exquisite surge of elation called success.

"You've done an amazing job." Anne turns to the entire room and applauds. "You've all done a fantastic job. I can't thank you enough. Call Dean and Deluca. Lunch is on me."

Now it's the turn of the dozen motley designers and computer nerds to applaud. Just at that moment the front door opens and a three-year-old boy wearing denim overalls rushes up to Nikki.

"Mommy! Mommy!"

Nikki sweeps him up and tosses him in the air. "Hey there, Tiger Balm. Justin, this is Anne."

Justin says "Hi" and sticks out his arm. Anne shakes his tiny hand.

"We went on the Staten Island Ferry," Justin says.

"No kidding, sailor." Nikki looks about to burst with maternal pride.

"It was rough out there," Justin announces.

"Well, it's a windy day."

"Choppy," Justin corrects.

A woman in her mid-thirties, athletic, wearing black jeans and a T-shirt, walks into the office and gives Nikki a spousal kiss.

"Lisa, this is Anne Turner. Lisa Lewis."

Lisa and Anne share a firm handshake.

"If *Home* gave frequent buyer miles, we could trek to Timbuktu. And that was *before* you hired Nikki. What a pleasure," Lisa says.

"Well, Nikki has done a fantastic job with the website," Anne says, feeling an immediate rapport with this loving and enthusiastic family. With it comes a twinge of longing.

"Let's go to lunch. I want focaccia!" Justin says.

"Only a downtown kid, huh?" Nikki says.

"Hey Justin, get a load of this!" a voice calls from the other end of the office. Anne turns to see a giant plastic firefly sailing through the air.

"Wow!" Justin screams, charging off.

"I didn't know," Anne says, nodding in Justin's direction.

"The crazy part is we didn't want a kid, a couple of hip downtown career dykes like us. But Lisa had this cousin in Oregon she'd never met," Nikki explains.

"Heroin addict, prostitute. Who'da thunk it? Oregon. She was Justin's mom," Lisa says.

"She died of an overdose. Justin was in the bed with her."

Anne tries to imagine the horrific scene. "How old was he?"

"Eight months. We got him three months later."

"Nobody knows who his father is," Lisa adds.

"Has he asked?"

Lisa nods. "And we told him the truth."

Anne turns and looks at the boy, who is gleefully launching another firefly. "He's a very lucky child," she says.

"No. We're the lucky ones," Lisa says.

Their marriage seems so guileless, so free of hidden agendas. Suddenly Anne feels dizzy and slightly faint. This is followed by a wave of nausea—they've been coming with some regularity for the past week.

"May I use your office for a moment?" she asks.

"Of course."

Anne retreats to the sanctuary of Nikki's large cluttered office. She sits down and stretches her legs out and waits for the nausea to pass. How would a child affect her marriage? Would the rivalries and resentments fade in the face of a new life? Or would the kid just become one more thing to struggle over?

And what would the baby look like, with its chubby little limbs? Would it have Charles's smile? His eyes? Her coloring? If so, they'd have to buy sunblock by the gallon. Then it floods back— that afternoon on John Farnsworth's leather couch, his flabby white body, his fat stubby penis poking into her, his tongue on her neck and cheek. She presses her fingertips into the knot of self-hatred at the back of her neck. She takes out her cell phone and gets Directory Assistance, then punches another number.

"Planned Parenthood." The voice sounds so reassuring.

"Yes, I wonder if you could answer a question for me."

"I'd be more than happy to try."

"Is it possible to determine a fetus's father?"

"It is."

"How is it done?" she asks, reaching for pen and paper.

"Through DNA testing of either the amniotic fluid or the chorion, which is the outer lining of the sac surrounding the embryo."

"And then that DNA is compared to the DNA of the possible father?" Anne asks.

"Exactly. How far along is the pregnancy?"

"About ten weeks."

"In that case, the chorionic villus sampling would be indicated. It's too early for amniocentesis. Of course, you'll need a blood sample from the possible father."

How is she going to get a blood sample from Charles?

"How long does it take to get the results?"

"About two weeks. The cost is around a thousand dollars. The company that performs the testing will coordinate the arrangements with your doctor."

She can't possibly go to her own gynecologist. Judith Arnold's husband is a publishing executive; they travel in overlapping social circles with Anne and Charles.

"Oh, one last question."

"Shoot."

"How much of the father's blood is needed?"

"Usually they take a syringe full, but all the lab really needs is a few drops."

After she hangs up, Anne realizes her nausea is gone. There's a knock on the door.

"Anne, lunch is here."

Anne joins the crew as they eagerly unload the shopping bags full of scrumptious goodies from Dean and Deluca. Suddenly she's famished. She finds a smoked turkey and roasted red pepper hero. There's a tug on her pant leg.

"Where's my focaccia?" Justin asks.

Anne digs into one of the bags and finds a thick slice of focaccia baked with mozzarella and sun-dried tomatoes.

Anne kneels down beside the boy. "Here you go, buckeroo."

"That's a silly name. Are you a silly lady?"

Anne looks up at Nikki.

"I guess I am a silly lady sometimes." Anne laughs.

"Silly like a fox," Nikki says.

14

AFTER WAKING FROM a deep nap, Emma walks to the corner bodega. She loves the smells in the cramped store: something fried and spicy, the dirt on root vegetables she's never seen before, city cats. She gathers up two apples, two oranges, a can of spaghetti, tea bags, milk, a box of Fig Newtons.

On her way home she passes a botanica. She stops and looks at the plaster figures in the window: Jesus, the Virgin Mary, an array of heroic saints in heroic poses. Gaudily painted, they remind her of what you can win at the county fair ball-toss on a dusty August night if you have a boyfriend. At the fair, the plaster figures aren't religious; they're dogs and cats and Elvis Presley and all around the lights of love swirl and there are pink puffs of cotton candy and whirligig music and farm folks strolling and show animals lazy in the night air. Emma hates the county fair.

As she walks into the botanica the fat proprietress—in a thin red dress stretched so tight across her front that her bosom is mashed down and indistinguishable from the other rolls of flesh—narrows her eyes.

"You have trouble," the woman states, certain as a judge. She lights an unfiltered cigarette.

"What kind of trouble?" Emma asks.

"Bad trouble," the woman says. She taps her temple and exhales by opening her mouth and letting the smoke billow out.

The store is heavy with smells, a thousand perfumes and incense sticks, the fresh layered over the stale in a dense mix that suddenly makes Emma dizzy. More plaster figures, their deadpan faces betraying no religious ecstasy, fill the shelves. And candles, hundreds of candles in glasses covered with saints and Jesus again. Jesus is everywhere in the botanica.

"I have magic for trouble," the woman says, holding out a small glass vial.

Emma takes the vial and stares at the light brown liquid it holds. "What will it do?"

"Make you safe."

"How much?"

"Twenty dollars."

Emma starts to unscrew the cap.

"No!" the woman warns. "On your door make a cross with it and sprinkle it all around your bed."

Emma hands the woman twenty dollars. Suddenly she wants to get out of the suffocating store. The plaster figures look evil—passive spectators to the world's unspeakable acts. What do they care? They're saints; they've cashed in their chips. As she closes the door on her way out of the store, Emma hears the woman mutter something unintelligible, in Spanish, something that sounds to her like a curse.

Before she unlocks her door Emma opens the vial—the liquid has a sharp fusty odor—wets her fingertip and makes a cross on the door. Inside, she unloads the food. She loves the bare cabinets, their corners home to crumbly spots of rust, and the noisy refrigerator with the cracked handle. She wants her apartment to be a refuge replete with books and teas and at least two different kinds of cookies. A safe place.

She moves the chair close to the window and eats the apple and then four Fig Newtons, savoring every grainy bite, as she watches the street life below. Across the street an old man sits in a lawn chair in front of his building; couples out for dinner stroll by; clutches of hip young people in black, long-limbed and laughing, ramble down the block. Emma finds the passing parade hypnotic, and a sweet fatigue comes over her. She sprinkles the rest of the magic water around her bed, crawls in, and reads *Heart of Darkness* until her eyes begin to hurt. She turns off the bedside lamp. Red light filters in from the neon sign and plays against the far wall. She can hear the distant muttering of a thousand voices, a thousand beautiful anonymous voices. Emma lies still for a long time, looking at the light and listening to the voices. She has always imagined her father living in a room like this.

It was a winter-weary day in March, filled with dirty snow and bare trees, and nine-year-old Emma was in no hurry to get home from school. Home to the creaky apartment over the hardware store. She was chilly in her too big parka and slightly soggy boots, but that didn't keep her from walking slowly, kicking her way down the small-town streets. The first thing she noticed as she climbed the stairs was that it was quiet; there was no music—no Janis, no Billie, no Piaf. Her mother always played music in the afternoon, singing along as she drifted from room to room getting higher and higher, changing her outfits, touching up her makeup, staring at the long-untouched painting on her easel.

The front door to the apartment was ajar. Emma pushed it open. Her mother was on the living-room floor wearing a hot pink top and her souvenir-of-Hawaii skirt, a panorama of paradise, her eye shadow smeared. She was staring into space—her skinny gaudy glamorous mother, her going-mad mother, sitting there splay-legged on some crazy mixture of Seconol and Vivarin and Valium, some crazy chemical cocktail concocted to dull her dreams. Emma knew immediately that he was gone, her sad-eyed father with his longing for golden California. Strangely enough, she was relieved. At least it was over. The screaming, the hitting, that awful dead feeling that permeated an apartment shared by two people who blamed each other for everything, whose every waking moment was an unspoken shout of "If only I hadn't met you."

Emma said nothing to her mother, but walked slowly into her bedroom and crawled under her bed. She pulled a towel over her and imagined her father making his way west, her pot-smoking, underground-comics-reading, incense-burning, bitterly unhappy father who loved Bob Dylan and Joni Mitchell and the Grateful Dead, off to seek his long-haired dream far from the dreary dying towns of western Pennsylvania. She imagined him in motels and rented rooms as he made his way across the country, she imagined him forgetting about his mistake, about his wife, his life, about Emma. She understood. And yet secretly, every time the phone rang, every time the mail came, she felt it—that strange sad tingle of hope.

Emma curls up into the fetal position on her bed. Fuck her father. He better not come around after she's famous, like one of those movie-star stories you read in the tabloids. His sorry ass won't get a dime out of her. Emma blows off that loser's memory and turns her thoughts to Charles Davis and his piney smell. She's seen men looking at her on the subway; she knows she's no dog. Her breasts are as pretty as Winona Ryder's. She lets her hands go up and explore them, running her fingertips in gentle circles. She's a goddamn survivor.

15

CHARLES IS RAVENOUS and he can feel the beginnings of a headache taunting him from behind his eyes. It isn't going well, the new book. Through the closed door, he hears Emma enter the outer office. With lunch, he hopes. She's a strange girl; he can't quite get a bead on her. Definitely not at home in her own body—today is the first day she's worn a skirt above her knees. Her figure is decent, small but well proportioned.

"Charles?" she says softly, tentatively, from behind the door. "Come in."

Emma pokes her head into the office. "I've got your veggie burger and carrot juice."

Charles gets up and joins her in the outer office. The crisp autumn air has brought up a touch of color on her pale skin and her eyes look especially bright. She smells faintly of peppermint soap. She hands him a tray loaded down with two hot dogs and a huge serving of french fries slathered with mayonnaise.

"I hope this is organic mayonnaise," he says, accepting the tray. "How's it going out here?"

"Steadily. How's it going in there?" Something in the way she asks, her serious curiosity, pleases him. He glances at the small V of flesh her open shirt affords.

"I'm trying to have faith in the process," he says. She nods—that grave, simpatico nod of hers that he finds so touching somehow. She has such lively brown hair. Why the hell does she keep it pulled back like that, and with a tacky red elastic band? She really is determined to downplay her charms. He wonders suddenly, Is she a virgin?

"Join me?" he asks.

"I won't interrupt your work?"

"I wouldn't have asked."

Emma picks up her salad and follows Charles into his office. He pulls up a chair for her. She bites her lower lip in exaggerated concentration as she squeezes orange dressing out of a small plastic packet. There's something so submissive about her, so yielding.

"That looks disgusting," he says about the Day-Glo dressing.

Emma looks over at his tray, brimming with grease and fat and hot dogs made of who-knows-what, and smiles slyly. When she smiles like that she becomes someone different—a mischievous little girl who cuts school to sneak into the movies. Maybe she isn't a virgin after all. Maybe she could teach him a trick or two. Not that he makes a habit of being unfaithful to Anne. In the twelve years of their marriage, there've been maybe half a dozen times, all when he was on the road and the opportunity was just too ripe to pass up—Charles flashes on that grad student in San Antonio who knocked on his door at two in the morning with a bottle of wine in one hand and a gram of coke in the other. Christ, she was hot. In awe of him. Like Emma. Like Anne.

"Did I get any interesting mail today?" he asks.

"There was one, from a woman in Colorado."

"Yes?"

"She wants to have your baby. She asked if you could send a specimen for in vitro fertilization."

"Believe it or not, I've had requests like that before. What did *I* tell her?"

"You told her you couldn't."

"Why not?"

That wily smile plays at the corners of her mouth again, and a flattering blush rises in her cheeks.

"Because . . . because you had a vasectomy five years ago."

"I beg your pardon?!"

"You told me to use my discretion. I figured she couldn't argue with . . . that."

He chuckles. "You're full of surprises, aren't you?"

Emma takes too big a bite of her salad. She sits with her back straight and her legs pressed together—a strange hybrid of re-pressed librarian and runaway street kid. Would she make love like a librarian—or like a street kid?

"Who *are* you? Tell me a secret," Charles says.

Emma reaches for a piece of bread, opens a tiny tub of butter, and methodically butters the bread. "I don't have any. I'm not exactly the stuff of great fiction," she says without looking up from her task.

"Let me see. . . . Grew up in a suburb of Chicago. Father a geology professor, mother a second grade teacher . . . only child . . . testing yourself in Manhattan before you go back for your degree in psychiatric social work."

Emma laughs. It sounds forced. She's so easy for him to rattle. He must remember that and be gentle with her. He imagines opening her blouse, lifting it off her shoulders.

"Well, I am an only child," she says.

"And the rest?"

"I had an uneventful childhood."

"There's no such thing as an uneventful childhood."

"I grew up in western Pennsylvania. Nothing but cows and coal mines. I suppose you could say I'm here in New York to test myself. I've always been fascinated by the city. And here I am.''

"Mom and Dad?''

"Just Mom and Dad.''

She pushes at her salad with her fork. Her shy evasions only increase his interest. They could knock off early one afternoon, have a few glasses of wine. He'd go slowly, never putting his pleasure before hers. Afterward she'd nestle her small body against his and they'd talk, share a sweet and tenuous intimacy. It could well develop into an affair. Just for a month or so, a month of sex and longing and solace.

"I'll tell you one thing, Mom never served mayonnaise with our french fries,'' Emma says.

"She didn't know what she was missing.'' He holds out the tray and she nibbles at a single fry.

"I still prefer tartar sauce,'' she says dryly.

Charles smiles at her and she returns his smile. There's a moment of silence, their eyes remain locked, and then she looks away.

Suddenly Charles wonders about her stability. She seems almost to be trying on different aspects of her personality as if they're hats and she isn't sure which ones fit. And something in the tightness that sometimes creeps into her voice hints at a well-concealed rage. This girl could be trouble, might do something inappropriate. He could see her, strung out and pathetic, accosting Anne in front of the building. Bad news. Emma is terrific as a secretary, but potentially disastrous as a lover. It's not worth the risk, not now. Just another distraction.

Emma reaches up and slowly traces her fingers down her neck. Is it an unconscious gesture? There's something undeniably erotic about it, and in spite of his admonition to himself, Charles feels his cock grow hard.

16

ANNE IS SITTING at her office desk leafing through the physicians listings in the Queens Yellow Pages. She comes across a women's health center—Dr. Milton Halpern, gynecologist-obstetrician, director.

There's a tap on the door. Anne quickly shuts the phone book and pushes it aside. "Yes."

Trent pokes his head in. "I'm off to lunch. Can I get you anything?"

"I'm fine, thank you, Trent."

When he's gone she calls the state medical board to see if Dr. Halpern has had any complaints lodged against him. None. She dials his office and requests an appointment.

"Have you seen the doctor before?"

"No."

"How is next Tuesday at ten-thirty?"

"Could he possibly fit me in this afternoon?"

"The doctor is fully booked."

"It's something of an emergency."

"All right, I'll book you in at the end of the day. Five-thirty."

"Thank you."

"Your name?"

"Kathleen Brody."

"Your phone number?"

Christ! Anne forgot they'd be asking for a phone number. Her mind races. She considers hanging up, then looks down at her phone. She reads the number aloud, transposing the last two digits.

"All right, we'll see you this afternoon. Do you know how to get here?"

"I'll find it."

Anne leaves the office at four, telling Trent she's getting a facial. She stops at an ATM and withdraws five hundred dollars and then walks briskly down Sixth Avenue to Thirty-fourth Street. Wedged between an electronics store and a McDonald's is a tiny wig shop. The interior is poorly lit and crowded with wigs on Styrofoam stands. The owner is an East Indian with a bored, leering manner. Anne points to a short brown wig cut in a pixie-ish Shirley MacLaine bob.

"Very nice wig," he says.

"May I try it on?"

"No. New York State law."

"Well, do you think it will fit me?"

"Okay, try it on."

Anne hastily pins up her hair and pulls on the tight cap and looks in the mirror. For a moment she doesn't recognize herself.

"Beautiful," the man says.

Anne pays for the wig and leaves the store with it on. She hails a cab and gives the driver the Queens address. As the car makes its way across the Fifty-ninth Street Bridge, Anne takes out her compact and with deft strokes applies foundation to her face. Then she darkens her eyebrows and puts on deep red lipstick.

The clinic is in Jackson Heights, a neighborhood Anne has
never visited before. She's surprised at how charming it is—tidy
tree-lined streets, graceful brick apartment houses. As they drive,
Anne picks out a suitable building and notes its number. The clinic
is in a low-slung building just off a slightly seedy shopping street.

The waiting room—worn gray carpeting, plastic chairs, posters
of Monet's water lilies—is a long way from Dr. Arnold's, with its
burnished wood and framed lithographs. Anne is glad there's no
one else waiting. The receptionist is a preoccupied Hispanic
woman. Anne quickly fills out the medical history form, listing the
address she noted on Elm Street. A dazed young Asian mother,
carrying one child and leading two others, comes out of the doctor's office and stops at the receptionist's desk. Anne begins to
sweat. Hillary Clinton is on the cover of *People*, but Anne barely has
time to pick up the magazine before a heavyset nurse with a
brusque maternal air leads her into an examining room. Anne sits
in a chair.

"What can we do for you today?"

"I'd rather discuss it with the doctor."

The nurse raises an eyebrow. "Are you pregnant?"

"I really would rather talk to the doctor."

"In that case, why don't you take off your clothes and put on
this gown?"

The nurse leaves. Anne has no intention of taking off her
clothes. The walls of the examining room are covered with bilin-
gual posters extolling proper pre- and postnatal care. There are
photographs of happy families enjoying their newborns. Anne wonders if she's doing everything she should be in terms of nutrition
and exercise. Oh, Christ, women have been having children for
thousands of years. She looks in the wall mirror, pats her dark hair.
There's a soft knock on the door and then it opens.

Dr. Halpern looks to be in his early sixties, with curly gray hair
and exhausted eyes. His shoes are scuffed.

"Milton Halpern."

"Kathleen Brody."

The doctor crosses his arms and leans against a counter. "What can I do for you, Mrs. Brody?"

Anne hears a baby crying in another room. She thought she was the last patient of the day. "I'm pregnant."

"Yes?"

Anne looks down, runs her fingers along the edge of the chair seat, exhales sharply. "I'm a married woman, and . . ."

Dr. Halpern takes a pen out of his breast pocket and starts to fidget with it. She looks at him. He holds her eyes and leans forward slightly.

"More than one man could be the father." Anne looks down at her hands. The polish on her left index finger is chipped.

The doctor takes a paper cup from a holder and fills it with water. He hands the cup to Anne. "These things happen," he says.

The clinic is overheated. No wonder she's sweating. She takes a drink of water. It's been ages since she's tasted tap water.

"I'm considering an abortion."

The doctor gives a small nod. "Do you have a regular gynecologist?"

"I do, but it's complicated. . . ." Anne finishes the water in a gulp. "Oh, Christ, how could I have done this to myself?"

"Are you taking anything for your anxiety?"

"Just something I picked up at the health food store."

"Does it help?"

"You should have seen me before."

The doctor chuckles.

Anne stands up. There isn't much room to move in the office. She sits back down. "I'd like DNA testing of the fetus. I want to know who the father is before I make any decisions."

"It's an expensive process. Does it really matter that much?"

"Yes. Will you help me?"

The doctor looks at Anne, studies her face. For a moment she's afraid he recognizes her.

"You're in your first trimester?"

"Yes."

"Well, chorionic villus sampling is not without risks. I won't recommend it without performing an examination and getting a full medical history."

"Fine. How soon could we schedule it?"

"Next week. As I'm sure you know, the lab will need a blood sample for DNA matching."

Anne nods. After her exam, she dresses and leaves, giving the receptionist the five hundred dollars as a deposit.

Anne walks into the apartment at 6:45 and heads for the master bedroom. In her closet, she pulls down an old hatbox, opens it, tucks the wig under the straw hat inside, and replaces the box. Her heart is thwacking in her chest. In the bathroom she picks up a glass and drops it. It shatters with a hollow sound that echoes off the room's tiles. She carefully picks up the shards of broken glass, leaving several on the floor, sharp and menacing. Deep in the bottom of the bathroom closet, on a shelf filled with half-used tubes of sunblock and hair conditioner, she stashes the vials Dr. Halpern's nurse gave her.

She heads for the kitchen. The door to Charles's domain is open, and she walks down the hallway. His outer office is deserted; the door to his inner office is closed. She listens: silence. She knocks lightly. "Charles?" No reply. Just as she's about to open the door, it opens from within and Emma emerges.

"He's gone out for a walk," the young woman says.

What was she doing in there? And with the door closed? Anne looks discreetly over Emma's shoulder. Everything looks in order. No Charles.

"Just my luck. The one day I get home at a decent hour. How's everything going here?"

"Just fine, for me. I hope I'm making things easier for Mr. Davis."

"I'm sure you are." Anne eyes Emma. She's wearing a hint of

makeup; she never did that when she was temping at *Home*. And those startling green eyes are so round and luminous.

"I saw the article about you in *In Style*," Emma says.

"Oh, God, they made me sound like a cross between Martha Stewart and Donatella Versace."

"Half the women I meet think you're the Messiah."

"That's my cue to say something terribly cynical and witty. But I won't." Anne has an ironclad rule never to condescend to her customers.

"How's everything at the office?" Emma asks.

"Chaotic."

"I hope that problem worked itself out."

"What problem?" Anne asks.

"You got a phone call that seemed to upset you. I think it was my second day working at *Home*. Anyway, it was raining."

Anne looks at Emma for a moment. Who is this girl? She walks past her, into Charles's office. She picks up his pack of Marlboros and takes one out, but doesn't light it.

"Unfortunately, many calls upset me these days. *Home* is about to go on-line. Getting there hasn't been easy. I probably should have kept you. You were good."

"It was a wonderful opportunity for me."

"Yes. And now you're here."

"I'm here."

Emma looks as if she's about to say something more and then thinks the better of it. What the hell was she doing skulking about in Charles's office?

"I was just on my way out," Emma says, gathering up her things. "Good night."

"Good night," Anne says. As she watches Emma walk down the hallway, Anne decides she wants her out of her house.

Back in the kitchen, Anne pours herself a glass of wine and finishes it in three sips. One glass won't hurt the baby. Hell, her mother swears she drank two gin and tonics every night when she was pregnant with Anne. She opens the fridge and checks on the chicken she's marinating in beer and curry and horseradish. They'll eat at the small table in the library, at the window overlooking the park. She'll put on Coltrane. And after dinner she'll run Charles a hot bath. . . .

The kitchen phone rings.

"Hello."

"Why haven't I heard from you, Annie? I've left three phone messages and two E-mails."

"Need you ask?"

"Don't give me that crap. You think my job is a day at the beach? I'm a vice president of a television network, cookie honey sweetie baby."

Anne laughs—who else could make her laugh at this moment?

"I miss you, Kayla."

Kayla Edelstein is Anne's best buddy. They were roommates at Stanford, two eighteen-year-olds from opposite ends of the continent who joyously discovered that they shared a sense of humor, passionate liberal politics, and enough drive to light Cleveland. After graduation they moved to Manhattan together, shared a basement apartment off Riverside Drive, dated and sometimes bedded a series of gorgeous young men, and dived full-tilt-boogie into their careers. Anne got her first job as an editorial assistant at *Vogue*, Kayla hers as an agent's assistant at William Morris. Within three years Kayla relocated to L.A., where her rise has been steady and sure. She's currently head of development for the country's second-largest cable network. The two friends speak at least once a week and make sure they see each other three or four times a year.

"So how are you?" Kayla asks in a voice that says, Don't try to bullshit me, kiddo.

"Good."

There's a long pause.

"All right, it's been a lousy couple of weeks."

"I've seen the reviews. Is he totally flipped?"

"Pretty much. I know you think he's a bulldog, and sometimes he is. But he feels things more acutely than most people. He can't help himself. It's part of what makes his work so good. And so difficult for him."

"Why don't the two of you come out here, lie by the pool in Santa Monica for a week? You need to get out of that town."

"Charles is throwing himself into a new book. It's the best thing. He knows he's capable of more than *Capitol Offense.* I don't care about his sales anymore. I just want him to tap into that magic again; I want him to be great again."

"So do I, Annie. What about your website? Am I going to love it?"

"You're going to way love it. It's the coolest. Sales are going to go through the roof."

"Why do I get the feeling there's something you're not telling me?"

"Because you have a very vivid imagination."

"If I had a very vivid imagination, would I be in television? What I do have is intuition, and it tells me you're holding back."

Anne drums her nails on the countertop. Should she tell her best friend about the shards of glass waiting for Charles on the bathroom floor?

"Maybe I *should* come out there for a couple of days," Anne says.

"Pretty please. I could use you right now. I just dumped Fred."

"But you adored him."

"I adored his demented sense of humor and the way he nibbled my inner thighs. What I didn't adore was the fact that he couldn't keep his dick in his pants."

"You told me he wasn't like that."

"*He* told *me* he wasn't like that. But my intuition didn't believe him. So I made some discreet calls and met this fabulous call girl–slash–private eye, Sorbonne grad, could be running Paramount but has this Jane Bond lifestyle she loves. Anyway she lured old Freddy into a zipless fuck, and believe me, it wasn't hard. Best five grand I ever dropped.''

"I'm sorry, Kayla.''

"I'm not. I'm thrilled. Saved by the babe.''

"But you really liked the guy.''

There's a long pause and Anne can almost hear Kayla's bravado fizzle.

"Yeah, you're right, I did. He was so funny. And nerdy. I guess even geeks can be shits. Oh, Anne, I'm thirty-seven and I've never had a stable relationship,'' Kayla says in a voice that's starting to crack.

"You will, honey, you will. And, hey, what about our friendship?''

"You're right. And fuck it—self-pity is the biggest bore.''

"Damn straight. Remember our solemn oath: We will never feel sorry for ourselves. We will always have a cleaning lady, and—''

"Sex is for *our* pleasure,'' Kayla finishes. The two friends break into laughter.

"Oh, God, Annie, I miss you.''

Anne hears the front door open. "Listen, I should run. I'll call you in a couple of days. Love you.''

"Oh, the genius just walked in? You're still a lovesick pup at heart, aren't you? Charles Davis *über alles*.''

Dinner doesn't go as Anne hoped. In spite of the Coltrane and the candles, the mood is about as romantic as a trip to the dry cleaners. Charles is tense and uncommunicative; he has three drinks and only picks at his food. Anne tries—a little too hard—to keep things warm and lively, bringing up the latest movies and political gossip, but it's obvious that he's bored and distracted. When she raves about her website she's rewarded with a condescending "Terrific.'' She feels like telling him he'd better hope the website is a success because his royalties on *Capitol Offense* sure as hell aren't going to pay for the apartment. She curses herself for buying into his sulk, is too wound up to eat, keeps flashing on the shards of glass, and her left foot won't stop twitching.

"Charles, why don't we get away, maybe down to Saint Bart's, even just for a long weekend?"

He finishes his drink and looks out the window. "You've got to stop crowding me, Anne."

"I wasn't aware that I *was* crowding you."

"You can't help it. You're just so full of enthusiasms. Sometimes they're hard to take."

"Our marriage is one of my enthusiasms. Perhaps it's a misplaced one."

"At the moment it may well be."

"What the hell is that supposed to mean?"

"It means that right now I'm consumed by my own struggle and incapable of giving you the attention you deserve. Maybe I should rent a little apartment in Rome for a year."

Wonderful—the great novelist spends a year in a garret overlooking the Tiber while she sweats it out in New York.

"Don't expect me to be here when you get back," Anne says.

Charles gets up and crosses the room. He lifts a painted Balinese monkey off the mantel and stares at its screeching face. "Only one thing is going to save me, to save *us*, Anne, and that's a great book. We have to work as a team. I need your help."

Anne goes around the room turning off the lights until the only illumination is the reflected glow that pours through the windows from the city outside. She stands in the middle of the room and steps out of her dress. Charles is watching her. She slips out of her bra and stands there in her soft cotton panties in the beckoning light. She knows that he still loves her body.

"Let's make love," she says.

Charles just stands there, looking at her. She can see it in his eyes—desire, faint at first, but building.

She goes to him and kisses him. "Please, darling, let's forget about the world for a little while. Let's get back to you and me."

She pulls off his jacket and runs her hands down his shoulders. Then she unbuttons his shirt, her fingers trembling lightly. She can smell his pine soap, his sweat, the wine on his breath. She pushes his shirt open. She touches his chest, his neck, the warmth under his arms. His eyes are half closed.

Slowly, very slowly, he moves an index finger down the curve of her breast. "You and me?"

"Yes," Anne whispers.

Charles leans in to kiss her, slipping his hands down the back of her panties and pushing them off her hips, taking control.

They met at a benefit softball game in Bridgehampton. She was twenty-three, winning raves from her bosses at *Vogue*, besieged by suitors, adoring the East. He was thirty-six, tanned and famous, and when he hit that triple and slid into third base, she was gone. They had a few cursory dates, but they both knew what those were about—prolonging the tension, foreplay basically. When they finally fell into each other's arms—in a bedroom that looked out on the endless dunes of the Hamptons, the Atlantic glistening beneath a billion stars—it was what she'd been waiting for all her life.

They got married three months later—at City Hall in Asbury Park, New Jersey, just for the hell of it. The first years were bliss. And it wasn't just the sex. It was exploring hidden corners of Brooklyn on windy Saturday afternoons, arguing over conceptual art at the Whitney, laughing at each other's imitations of dull or pompous people they met, spending long winter nights reading on the overstuffed sofas in the living room of their Turtle Bay apartment.

Charles was a red-hot ticket in those days, and he made furthering her career a personal crusade. Lunch with the president of Doubleday; dinner parties to introduce her to editors, photographers, and writers; high-profile literary and cultural events—*New*

York magazine named them one of the city's Ten Most Glamorous Couples. They got a good laugh out of that one. But it all paid off: within a year Anne had a contract to do the first of her popular coffee table books on the "art" of entertaining.

Anne thought their happiness would last forever. Although the erosion has been slow and steady, she has never looked at another man. Still does not want another man.

After their lovemaking—a fierce, greedy, almost impersonal bout—Anne gets up and walks to their bedroom. She brushes her teeth, being careful not to step on the broken glass. She suddenly feels guilty and ridiculous, almost bends down and sweeps up the shards—but no, she *must* know; it's that simple. She lies on the bed and pretends to study a contract. Where is Charles? The apartment is so quiet.

Then he materializes—like a ghost—in the doorway. Anne starts.

"Scare you?" Charles asks. He's naked and has a drink in his hand.

"You're so quiet." Even from across the room Anne can smell him, his after-sex smell, pungent and moist.

"Thinking. Thinking is quiet."

"What are you thinking about?"

"Shhhh." He puts a finger up to his lips. "Loose lips sink books."

"Ah."

"Going to go do some work," he says.

"Don't you want to shower?"

"Do I stink?"

"No."

"Yes, I do. I stink."

"Well, if you stink, why don't you shower?"

"Probably because you suggested it."

Anne glances over to the bathroom. She gets out of bed and

goes to him, puts her arms around his neck and kisses him softly on the lips. She presses her body, her hips, against his. "Or we could take one together. Who knows what might develop?"

"Oh, no, I've had too much to drink. You're right, though, I do stink. A nice long shower and I'll be good as new."

Anne stops breathing as she watches him walk into the bathroom. His feet cross the black-and-white tiles, he's heading right for the glass—he misses it. Her breath escapes in a rush.

Then he turns to grab a washcloth.

"Shit." He turns his foot up and blood is running from the cut.

"What is it, darling?" Anne says, going to him. "Oh, no." A shard of glass is sticking out of the sole of his foot. "Let me get it."

She kneels and pulls out the thin shard and then squeezes his foot, watching as large drops of blood fall onto the tiles. "I dropped a glass earlier, I was sure I got it all up. I'm sorry. You get in the shower, I'll clean this up."

" 'Tain't nothin'," Charles mutters before stepping into the stall. Anne opens the closet door, ostensibly to reach for a sponge. She leaves the door open, blocking Charles's view, and retrieves a vial. She gingerly uses a piece of glass to push several drops of blood into the vial, her heart hammering in her chest. She puts the stopper in the vial and quickly wipes up the rest of the blood. Then she walks quickly to the kitchen, opens the refrigerator, takes out her box of Maison du Chocolat chocolates—Charles hates them, eats only Hershey bars—and slips the vial under the top layer. Then she savors a cocoa-dusted truffle.

17

ANNE TURNER IS MURDERED—stabbed to death in broad
daylight by an escaped mental patient, right on Fifty-seventh Street
in front of a crowd of horrified onlookers. The *Post* prints a front-
page photo of her body lying on the sidewalk, blood pooling beside
her, the wound on her neck dark and hideous. In the wrenching
months that follow, Emma is there for Charles. He comes to
depend on her, at first to handle all the prosaic details of his life,
but slowly his need becomes emotional. And then one day it goes
further—they make love, fall in love. He takes care of her, she
nurtures him, his writing regains its former power. They rarely go
out; it's just the two of them in this beautiful apartment. Marriage
becomes inevitable. On a perfectly ordinary morning, a Tuesday,
they go down to City Hall for the simple, poignant ceremony. She
becomes Mrs. Charles Davis—Emma Davis, Emma Davis, Emma
Davis. . . .

Emma drags herself back to reality and takes the rubber band
from around the thick pile of the day's mail. Suddenly there's a

jangling beside her ear. She looks up to see Charles standing in the doorway, holding a single key on a metal ring.

"See this key?"

Emma nods.

"I want you to take it and lock me in this room for six hours."

"Are you serious?"

"I don't want you to let me out, no matter how hard I scream, pound, or wail. Understood?"

Emma looks from the key to Charles. He actually wants her to do this. "All right," she says.

She takes the key. Charles walks into his office and turns. They look at each other. There's something in his eyes, something yielding, teasing, that excites Emma. She slowly closes the door, inserts the key, and turns it. An unfamiliar sense of power pours over her, of having control over another human being. She likes it. She sits down and attacks the mail.

Emma is completely absorbed in making notes to herself on a yellow legal pad when she hears a rapping on the door behind her.

"For Christ's sake, jailer, have you checked the time?"

Could six hours really have passed? Emma slips the pad into her bag and unlocks the door. Charles stands in the doorway, hands gripping the lintel above him, looking like an athlete who's just stepped off the field.

"How was it?" Emma asks.

"Excruciating . . . strange . . . maybe a little exciting."

Emma feels a blush rush up her body. She turns away from Charles and busies herself with some papers on her desk. "Your wife called. She won't be home for dinner."

"Then you and I will go out."

"Oh, no, that's all right, really," Emma says, making a great show of finding a letter on the desk and taking it to the file cabinet.

"Do you have other plans?"

"Well, not exactly," she says, searching through the file drawer for the right folder.

"Emma, we're going out to dinner."

The way he says it, that tone in his voice, the finality, the command. "I'm not very hungry," she mumbles, still paging through the drawer.

Charles leans in, forces her to meet his gaze. "Would you feel better if we went Dutch?"

"Probably."

"Dutch it is, then," he says, going to get his coat.

Emma closes the file cabinet, crumples up the letter, and drops it in the trash.

About twice a year Charles rides the subway, as much to remind himself that it still exists as to get to his destination. So when Emma insists that they not only eat on her turf but take her means of transportation to reach it, he's willing. Sitting beside her on the train, Charles feels loose, slightly ecstatic. The six enforced hours were good ones. The truth is, he didn't spend them writing. He pulled down a first edition of *Irreparable Damage*—the book that Emma loved so much—and reread it from beginning to end. He was caught up in the book in a way he hadn't expected to be, and now he feels inspired. But is it by his own words? Or by the young woman sitting beside him on this rocking train?

The Lower East Side, that city of ancient tenements, is a foreign land to Charles. As they walk down the battered streets, past old Jews, young Hispanics, and downscale artists, Charles is reawakened to what a huge and wondrous city he lives in. Emma leads him to a bare-bones Cuban restaurant tucked away on a teeming corner. They take a window booth and she orders for the two of them: avocado salad, black beans, yellow rice, and chicken that's been cooked in a chunky tomato-onion sauce until it falls from the bone, as tender as love. After savoring the earthy food, they sit and look out the window, slowly eating dessert—silky flan with a burnt-sugar bottom.

Charles feels that he's in a different world somehow, a place where he isn't Charles Davis, where he shucks that mantle, that burden, and is just another face on the street, just a man. He loves being led into this new land, eating this simple food. He can't remember the last time he's felt so unencumbered, as if he might be getting back to something important. He thinks of Portia, of how much she would enjoy this neighborhood, this restaurant, and, he ventures, this young woman.

"I'd forgotten how satisfying rice and beans could be," Charles says.

Emma smiles at him and, in the glow from the streetlight coming in through the window, he notes again what lovely lips she has, how sensual the lower half of her face is. There's even the hint of a pout about her mouth, a pout that the rest of her face isn't sure what to do with.

"I used to come to places like this when I first moved to New York and had about fifty cents to my name. Funny how you work your ass off until you've priced yourself out of the things you really love," Charles says.

"Sometimes I sit here for hours, just looking out the window. I find it soothing."

"That's the first time I've heard the Lower East Side described as soothing."

"It's the anonymity. I love the feeling in New York of being invisible. Small towns can suck the life out of you."

"So can big towns. Be careful, little girl."

"But don't you find it stimulating? As a writer? I mean, look at those two."

Charles follows Emma's gaze out the window to a storefront across the street where a raven-haired middle-aged woman in stretch pants and flip-flops is exchanging heated words with a much younger man with slicked-back hair and a gold stud in one ear. Charles watches them for a moment.

"A lonely woman and her Don Juan son," he says. "He hasn't been home in three days. She's telling him she's been tearing her hair out, lighting candles at church. What she really means is that she's insane with jealousy that some other woman is more important to him than she is."

Emma considers Charles's words for a moment, not taking her eyes off the couple. "I think they're lovers," she says.

"You do?"

"I think she's married to a seventy-year-old grocer who brought her here from Santo Domingo. She has a Pekingese and a pet hen she keeps in a cage in the kitchen. One morning she was walking the dog in the rain and decided to take him around the block again even though her umbrella was broken and her hair was getting wet. The young man was coming out of a coffee shop—the one he eats at every morning, even though the food is bad."

"Why does he keep eating there?" he asks.

"He's a creature of habit. There she was with the Pekingese, her hair plastered down with the rain. Something about her touched his heart—the shoes she was wearing, the way one spoke of her umbrella was bent out of shape. He knelt on the sidewalk and petted the dog. Rain soaked through his T-shirt. He looked up at her and he was lost."

"Why lost?"

"Because he knows he'll never forget her. On his deathbed it's her face he'll see. He wants her to leave her husband, but she can't. He's seventy, he brought her here, there's the hen. She's telling her lover to leave her, even though every drop of blood in her body wants him."

Charles looks at the couple and sees what Emma sees.

"Is there a happy ending?" he asks.

"He'll leave her. His pride. He'll marry a younger woman, move to Brooklyn; they'll have babies. One day he'll be in the city. He'll see her across the street, walking her dog. Her hair will be gray, but he won't notice. His heart will stop. It might start to rain."

Emma has lost all self-consciousness, is radiant in the dim light of the coffee shop. Her story over, she's quiet for a moment. Across the street, the couple is gone. Emma turns and looks at Charles, as if she is stepping out of another world. She is suddenly aware of herself again, and her small frame stiffens.

"I want to see where you live," he says.

18

IN QUEENS, Anne lies with her robe open on the hospital examining table, wondering why she doesn't feel more vulnerable. The doctor, young and intense, has injected the local anesthetic into her belly, and she can feel the area growing numb. The vial containing Charles's blood sits on the nearby countertop. How dark and thick blood is.

"Are you all right, Mrs. Brody?" the doctor asks.

"Fine, thank you."

"I'm going to put some petroleum jelly on your stomach in preparation for the ultrasound," he says.

Anne feels the texture of the cold jelly as the nurse spreads it. Then the doctor begins to run a metal wand over her stomach. Anne looks over at the monitor and sees the embryonic life growing inside her. She reaches out and squeezes the nurse's hand. She's immediately embarrassed by her gesture and withdraws her hand. The nurse pats Anne's arm.

The nurse takes the ultrasound wand from the doctor and he picks up a long needle.

"Please," Anne says. "Be careful."

The doctor gives her a calm smile. Dr. Halpern has assured her of his expertise. Anne determines right then and there to stick with Dr. Halpern if she decides to have the baby. You don't have to be rich to get good medical care, she thinks, just lucky.

She turns her head away as he inserts the needle into her stomach.

"All done," the doctor says.

It's dark when Anne walks out onto the sidewalk and around the corner to the brightly lit commercial street. Evening shoppers are out in force and she joins the throng. She has a sudden craving for peanut butter cookies and she ducks into the nearest grocery and buys two packs, one of which she tears open and begins to devour even as she waits in line to pay.

19

CHARLES AND EMMA walk under the cloudy night sky, toward Chinatown.

"Don't expect much," she says as they reach the old brick building. Emma unlocks the front door and begins to climb the stairs; Charles follows close behind. Her anxiety increases with each step. *Stay calm, you've come this far. Stay calm.*

Emma opens the door and Charles follows her inside. The restaurant's neon sign bathes the room in a dim crimson glow. She turns on a light and stands expectantly while Charles looks around. The Saturdays she's spent combing the thrift shops and sidewalks of lower Manhattan have yielded eclectic treasures. The fruit crates cribbed from the Chinese grocer are filled with thirdhand books. A fringed shawl is draped over her bed. There's a Persian rug worn through in several places, a lamp in the shape of three puppies, an old manual typewriter, a wedding photo of a handsome black couple circa 1910. Her plates and glasses are mismatched and colorful. Until now Emma was proud of her apartment, but suddenly—with

Charles Davis there—it looks shabby, depressing, a place where a crazy girl trying to pass for normal might live.

Emma drops her coat and bag on the bed and goes to the stove. "Can I make you a cup of tea?" She can feel him behind her, standing there, judging her, seeing her for who she is. She fills the kettle with water. The first patter of raindrops sounds against the roof above them. She turns and he's staring at her.

"What?" she asks. "What is it?"

"Nothing." Then he smiles gently, almost tenderly. "I was just admiring your apartment."

"I have Earl Grey and some lovely jasmine I found on Mott Street. Very intense," Emma says, grateful to have something to actually *do*. She opens the tin of jasmine tea; its sweet exotic fragrance drifts up into the air. Charles leans in to smell the tea and as he does, he gently touches her hand.

"I'd better stick with the Earl Grey," he says.

Emma turns and reaches for the box of tea bags. She wishes he'd chosen the jasmine, it requires more steps to prepare, would have given her more excuses to avoid looking at him. Reaching for two mugs, she knocks over a small plant, a sad little mum she bought on impulse and couldn't bring herself to throw away after its single bloom died. The plant falls to the floor, spilling dirt. Emma lets out a little cry. She's such a pathetic little fuckup. She falls to her knees to clean up the mess. Charles kneels beside her.

"I'm making you uncomfortable, aren't I?"

"I'm sorry. I don't have many visitors."

"I'll take care of this. You get the tea."

She stands up and busies herself with the tea while he cleans up the plant.

"I'm afraid this plant has had it," he says.

"With my brown thumb, I'm amazed it's lasted this long."

As she pours the boiling water into the mugs, she notices that he's crossing the room, approaching her dresser. He picks up the framed photo, the one photo she treasures above all others, the one photo she didn't want him to notice.

"You and your father?" he asks, holding up the faded color print of Emma and her stoned, long-haired father on the beach at Lake Canoga—scruffy, weedy Lake Canoga—her father with his goofy smile, his proud, goofy smile, proud of his nine-year-old princess, his baby, his Emma. She remembers that day so vividly, just the two of them driving through the hills to the lake, her daddy getting stoned, reaching over and rubbing her head, singing along with Crosby, Stills, Nash, and Young: "Teach your children well. . . . Feed them on your dreams . . . and know they love you."

But then he fucked her over. Too bad. So sad.

"You look like him," Charles says.

"Do I?"

"What does he do?"

"I don't know. Four months after that picture was taken, he left us."

"Just left?"

"He went to work and never came back."

"That must have been tough."

Tough. "How do you like your tea?"

"Straight up. Do you have any pictures of your mother?"

Emma brings Charles his mug of tea and makes a point of sitting in the chair farthest from him.

"I wish I had some cookies to offer you," she says.

"Do you have any pictures of your mother?" Charles repeats.

"My mother? She keeps promising to send me one, but she's so busy," Emma says as casually as she can.

"Remarried?"

"Yes." All these questions make Emma want to scream. Instead she folds her hands in her lap and takes the plunge. "I have a confession to make."

Charles looks at her expectantly.

"I'm a closet smoker. Could you hand me my bag?"

Charles reaches for Emma's bag, spilling its contents. A yellow legal pad covered with writing tumbles out, followed by cigarettes, elastic hair bands, a subway map, and a battered copy of *Play It as It Lays*. Charles picks up the pad. Emma leaps up from her chair and grabs it from him.

"What's wrong?" he asks.

"Nothing," Emma says, wrapping her arms around the pad.

"You're making me very curious."

Oh good. "It's nothing," Emma says, returning to her chair.

Charles's questioning eyes bore into her. "It's an awfully important nothing."

"Oh, all right. Really, it's just something I wrote, am writing . . . I don't know."

"So you're a closet writer, too."

"I guess. Not a very good one. Now can we change the subject?"

"Let me see it," he says.

Emma pretends she's considering it.

"Let—me—see."

And so she does. Charles begins reading. Emma feels goose bumps break out on her arms and neck. Without taking his eyes off the page, he settles into the armchair. The room grows very still. Emma is at a loss as to what to do with herself. He's reading so intently. She walks as quietly as she can over to the window. Across the street, a cat crouches in the gutter devouring a scrap of food. The New York night feels full of promise, a sea of warm hope delivering Emma from her pain, carrying her to her fate. She turns. Charles is still reading, bathed in the soft lamplight, his lips slightly pursed. He flips a page, and then another. Finally Emma can stand it no longer.

"May I have it back, please?"

He cuts her off with a brusque "shhhhh" and keeps reading until he reaches the end. He looks up at her. "Is this part of something longer?"

"I don't know. I guess so."

"You guess?"

"There's more. There's a lot more."

"Would you let me see it?"

"Charles, you don't have to——"

"Read anything I don't want to. I know that, Emma. But I want to read more of this."

Emma goes to her dresser and takes out the pages she's been writing for so long now. All but the most recent are neatly typed. Her book, her story, her life. She feels the weight of the pages in her hand and then, hesitantly, gives them to Charles.

"Do you mind if I take these home tonight?"

Emma shakes her head.

As they finish their tea, Charles, leaning forward in his chair, tells her about showing his first novel to his writing teacher at Dartmouth. Of how he didn't sleep for two days while she read it. Emma nods and smiles but finds it hard to pay attention.

"Walk me downstairs," he says.

It's cool out; the rain has stopped. Charles cradles the stack of papers and hails a cab. He squeezes Emma's shoulder and says, "See you in the morning."

Emma watches the cab pull out into traffic and disappear up the street.

It's going to happen.

20

ANNE IS PROPPED UP in bed, going over a licensing agreement with a small Vermont furniture maker. She's having a hard time concentrating. The numbness is gone from her stomach; there's just a tiny point of tenderness where the needle went in. For a five-hundred-dollar surcharge the company doing the DNA testing agreed to expedite her tests; she'll have the results in about ten days. She reaches for another disgusting peanut butter cookie and picks up her bedside phone and dials.

"Hello."

"Kayla, it's me."

"I hate you. I spent eighteen hundred dollars today on your goddamn website."

"Isn't it great?"

"It's amazing! Just what I need—a whole new way to shop. You're a genius. And where did you find those gold-leaf tiles?"

"Deepest Brooklyn."

"Wow. But I'm canceling the whole order if you don't tell me what's bugging you. Right now."

Anne puts her paperwork on the bedside table. She lifts off the covers and sits on the edge of the bed.

"I'm pregnant . . . and Charles may not be the father."

There's a long pause.

"Sorry. I was picking my jaw up off the floor. Tell me *everything*."

And Anne does, spewing out the whole story. When she's done she feels better than she has in months.

"That motherfucker Farnsworth," Kayla says.

"No, Kayla, that's too easy. I could have stopped it."

"He shouldn't have put you in that position. But that's a moot point. What are your thoughts about the baby?"

"Even if it is Farnsworth's, I don't know if I can go through with an abortion. There's a life growing inside me."

"What about *your* life, Anne? If it's Farnsworth's, there's a chance you'll hate the baby. Think about the ramifications of that. You know I'm still a little conflicted about my own abortion, but at the same time I know I did the right thing. I've never doubted it for a second. It wasn't the right time and it wasn't the right man. The same may be true for you."

"But it is the right time. I want a child."

"But do you want *this* child?"

Anne starts to pace around the room. She looks down at the park, its lights twinkling in the dark. What fun it would be to take her little child—would it be a boy or a girl?—to the zoo and the carousel. To share a tuna fish sandwich sitting on a park bench.

"It's my child as much as the father's, Kayla. It's my baby."

"Anne, it's your decision and you're my best friend and I love you and I'll support you in whatever you decide. But remember that you have choices."

Anne imagines going to an Upper East Side clinic for the abortion, spending a couple of recuperative days at Canyon Ranch. The whole thing would be over with and she could get on with her life. It seems like such a simple solution. Especially considering the current state of her marriage.

"I'm speaking to a media buyers' convention in Scottsdale on Saturday. Why don't I fly to New York as soon as I'm done?" Kayla says.

An overwhelming sadness descends on Anne. She turns away from the window and sits on the floor, her back against the wall.

"Are you going to our fifteenth reunion?" she asks, knowing Kayla will grasp her need to change the subject.

"Hell, yes, it's the ultimate gloat fest. All those little blond chippies slaving away on Wall Street and in Silicon Valley. We showed 'em, didn't we, Turner?"

Anne leans her head against the side of her dresser and closes her eyes. "We showed 'em."

"I'm six hours away from buying you a big fat martini. Promise me you'll call if you want me to hop a plane."

"I promise."

"Love you, kiddo."

"I love you, Kayla."

Anne hugs her knees and rests her head on them. The room seems so big from down on the floor. She starts to hum to herself, some half-forgotten lullaby her father loved.

Then she hears the front door open, followed by Charles's approaching footfalls. She scuttles into the bathroom, stands up, and grabs her toothbrush. He appears in the bathroom doorway, his eyes shining.

"Hi," he says, giving her cheek a perfunctory kiss.

"Where've you been?"

"I took a long walk."

"Do you want me to heat something up?"

"I ate."

"Oh. Where?"

"I grabbed a bite at a coffee shop."

Charles hates coffee shops.

"I want to do some work," he says. He takes off his shirt and splashes cold water on his face and under his arms.

"Oh, Charles? How much longer do you think you'll need that secretary?"

"Hard to say." He walks over to his closet and puts on a worn denim workshirt.

Anne stands in the bathroom doorway. "But you want to keep her around?"

"It's nice to know she's out there staying on top of things."

"I see."

"You don't mind, do you?"

"A little."

"Why?"

"I don't trust her."

"What's not to trust? She's just some highly efficient, highly insecure girl."

There's a moment of silence.

"It's a nice night out," Charles says.

"Are you on to something?"

Charles nods but doesn't elaborate.

"Well, that is exciting. Although it's not easy being a literary widow."

"Think how much fun it'll be when I return from the grave."

21

WALKING DOWN THE HALLWAY that leads to Charles's offices, Emma takes several deep breaths and tries to put a casual, everyday expression on her face. She walks into the outer office and there he is, sitting at her desk, her pages in front of him.

"Do you know the ending?" he immediately asks. He looks as if he's gotten very little sleep.

"I think so."

"Don't tell me." Charles looks down at the pages for a long moment, then crosses to Emma and takes her by the shoulders. "It's extraordinary, Emma."

Emma feels light-headed, as if all the blood has drained from her body and been replaced by a rush of pure oxygen. "You don't have to say that."

"How long have you been working on this?"

"About two years."

"Have you taken writing classes?"

"No." He's looking at her so strangely, holding her shoulders so tightly. "I wrote in school. I won a story contest in the eighth grade."

"When do you write?"

"Whenever I can." Emma makes a small move to get away. "Shall I make coffee?"

He gives a little snort, as if coffee is the most insignificant thing in the world. He finally lets go of her and walks across the room, rubbing his hands together. Then he spins around. "I'd like you to finish it here."

"What?"

"I want you to finish your book here."

"But the job—"

"Your job description just changed. This would help me a thousand times more than all the answered letters and returned phone calls in the world. I want these two rooms to be charged with electricity, with creative fire." He gestures to her manuscript. "This is the whole fucking ball game."

"But, Charles . . ."

He crosses back to her and lifts her chin. His voice becomes low and intimate and warm, like . . . like a father's. "Listen to me, Emma. When I was just about your age, someone helped me. I'd like to give it back. I don't want you to think too much about what I'm going to say—I just want you to keep on doing exactly what you're doing—but you have a gift, a wonderful gift."

Emma feels a sudden urge to lay her head on his shoulder and have him stroke her hair. She wants him to take care of her, to guide her, to make the world a safe place, finally, at least for a little while.

"What do you think? You and me, these two rooms?"

Emma nods.

"Good. Let's get to work."

22

CHARLES AND EMMA are walking across Central Park on their way to the movie theater. After a week of nonstop work, he's insisted they take the afternoon off, feels it's important for her to see *Rashomon*. He leads her along his favorite path, the one that winds through the Shakespeare Garden, planted with flowers mentioned in the plays, and then up a hill to Belvedere Castle. There's a courtyard beside the castle and they lean against its low stone wall and admire the view of northern Manhattan and the little lake that sits below, beside an outdoor amphitheater where Shakespeare is performed on summer nights.

"Next year we'll go to one together," he says.

"Won't that be a midsummer night's dream," Emma says and then wishes she hadn't.

Charles smiles. "Come on, we don't want to miss the beginning of the movie."

Emma loves sitting beside Charles in the dark theater—the forced intimacy, their shoulders touching, the large bag of popcorn they're sharing. She's enthralled by Kurosawa's artistry, by the story, the *stories*, he's telling. Charles is like a little boy showing off a treasured possession.

"He uses the camera like a paintbrush—it's masterful."

Emma notices that nearby moviegoers are shooting him glances. Normally, she would have been mortified, but with Charles she doesn't care. She's never seen him so adorable. When she looks over, his eyes are dancing in the screen's reflected light.

"Every single frame has a purpose, just as every sentence should. You have to direct the reader's eye!"

"Shhh!" someone hisses.

Emma laughs nervously. Charles is momentarily chastened. They watch the film unfold in silence for a few minutes and then Charles can no longer contain himself.

"This is the kind of control I want you to work for. By the way, your rewrite of the first chapter is brilliant. I'm going to show it to my agent."

"Hey, c'mon," someone admonishes.

"All right, all right," Charles grumbles.

Emma sinks down in her seat, charmed by Charles's enthusiasm, embarrassed by his outburst, and stunned by his statement. Nina Bradley is going to read her work! In the darkness, Emma smiles to herself.

After the movie, they ride uptown in a cab. It's Emma's first taxi ride, and it feels luxurious, almost decadent. Outside the window the city passes by as if it too is a movie, unfolding for her personal pleasure. Charles has turned to face her and has an arm on the seat back. He keeps touching her lightly, on her knee, her shoulder.

And then, in a quiet, serious voice, he says, "Emma, the story you're telling—that young boy, his abusive mother—where did it come from?"

Emma doesn't turn to him, but keeps looking out the window as she speaks. She's been expecting this question. "There was this woman who lived with her son above the stationery store downtown. She was clearly disturbed. They were always dressed in dirty clothes, he was skinny and sad. Everyone in town talked about them, made fun of them behind their backs. One day I saw the two of them sitting at the lunch counter in Woolworth's. She was talking to herself while he sat there eating his grilled cheese sandwich, trying to pretend everything was normal. But there were tears in his eyes.''

"Most writers put a lot of themselves into their first books," Charles says gently.

"I'm probably no exception. After my father left, my mother started drinking and taking pills. I'm sure I saw myself in that little boy.''

They ride in silence for a few blocks. Emma can feel Charles studying her as she looks out the window.

"Is your mother better now?''

"Yes, she is.''

"You've gotten inside the boy's head. But don't back away from the horror of the situation. The mother may be sad, but ultimately she's a monster.''

"But I want her to be a human being first.''

"She is a human being, a human being who is destroying her own progeny. You can't pull back on that.''

Emma turns to him abruptly. "I have no intention of pulling back.''

They're both surprised by the power in her voice.

Emma laughs uneasily. "I just mean—''

"You don't have to tell me what you mean. . . . Emma, I've enjoyed our day together.''

Emma looks down at her hands and for a moment she's afraid she'll cry. Or throw up. She takes several deep breaths. "Thank you for everything, Charles.''

"Look at me.''

Emma slowly looks up.

"You're crying.''

"No, I'm not. I am not crying. I'm not.''

And then they're both laughing and the taxi feels like a boat on a starry-night sea and Emma, as she discovers a part of herself she didn't know existed, an elation as pure as light, almost stops watching herself, but can't quite, and so stores the moment for future remembrance.

23

IGNORING THE DASH to each season's trendy new restaurant, Nina Bradley can be found—winter, summer, spring, and fall—at her prime table at the Four Seasons. She understands the value of being seen and of seeing, and she enjoys the homage that she's paid by the steady stream of media, publishing, and entertainment people who come through the restaurant. A brief stop at Nina Bradley's table is a well-known New York ritual.

Nina, whose marriage to a much-too-dull businessman was, in her words, "a six-year cruise to nowhere," is far too set—and content—in her ways to waste time looking for another man. She spends most weekends at her farm up in Columbia County. She loves the place, which she has willed to the Nature Conservancy. She maintains it impeccably and is proud of the cattle her farm manager raises organically. Nina has an occasional affair, but at her age eligible men are hard to find, and frankly, she sometimes thinks they just aren't worth the trouble.

As Charles finishes up his steak, the waiter sets down Nina's black coffee and removes her half-eaten grilled vegetable terrine. It's been a good lunch. Something is definitely happening with Charles. She hasn't seen him quite this animated in years; his recent bitterness seems to have evaporated. If she didn't know better, she'd suspect he was in love. But it isn't that. He's being very cagey about his work, which is a good sign—he likes to surprise Nina.

"Thank God for our lunches. Anne never serves steak anymore," Charles says, savoring his last bite. Nina loves the unabashed pleasure he takes in food. She can appreciate good cooking, but as for swooning and swaying over the latest Moroccan cheese or Ecuadorian roast-goat recipe, well, count her out. At least Anne has a sense of humor about all the culinary chatter.

"I hadn't eaten a steak in two years when I bought my farm. Then I got to know a few cows and realized that any animal that dumb had to have been put on earth for man to eat," Nina says.

Charles looks at Nina with unabashed affection. The man is feeling good about something. "Any industry gossip?" he asks.

"Vera Knee just got four hundred grand for the paperback rights to *Honey on the Moon*." As soon as the words are out, Nina curses herself. Cows aren't the only dumb creatures, she thinks ruefully, and quickly tries to recover. "Of course, her book is completely unreadable. And I don't care if she got a cool million, I'm not interested in representing any of this recent crop of so-called writers with more personality than talent. I've got a stack of manuscripts this high in my office. I'm sending them all back unread."

"But what if there's one at the bottom of that stack that's the real thing?"

"Then I hope it lands on the desk of someone who cares," she says. "Will you excuse me, Charles." Nina gets up and heads toward the ladies' room to reapply her signature scarlet lipstick. She'll be good goddamned if she's going to switch to purple, no matter how hard MAC and *Essence* push it for black women. She thinks it looks like a bruise.

•   •   •

Charles watches as Nina walks across the restaurant, watches as heads turn ever so slightly. In a black silk blouse and tailored black slacks, she is unarguably the most striking woman in the restaurant. Charles wishes he could tell her about Emma. But Charles and Nina's relationship ends at a certain place, a place they both recognize and tacitly acknowledge, but never discuss. Friends to the death? Absolutely. Intimate? Never. Sometimes Charles wonders if she ever aches for someone to see her through the long night. But Nina knows what she's doing, knows all about trade-offs, knows that no one—least of all a black woman of her generation—reaches her level of success without paying a price. And it's a price Nina Bradley pays without a whimper or a whine.

Charles reaches into his briefcase and takes out a manila envelope. He opens it and lifts out a sheaf of manuscript pages. He reads the title page:

Chapter One

from

The Sky Is Falling

A novel

by

Emma Bowles

Charles thinks of Emma, imagines her up in his office at this very moment, bent over her desk, writing. He removes the title page and tucks it into the inside pocket of his jacket. Then he puts the pages back in the manila envelope. He wants to make sure Nina gives the chapter an unbiased reading. There's no way she'll miss Emma's talent and promise.

A ruddy-faced man in an expensive suit approaches the table. "Charles, how are you?"

Charles blanks. What is his name? . . . Arvin? Publicity director for a rival publishing company. A notorious boor.

"Hello, Arvin," Charles says, hoping Arvin has the class to heed his indifferent tone.

No such luck. "I thought you were treated very unfairly on *Capitol Offense*. It's a helluva book."

"Thanks."

"You know, I heard Vera Knee—"

"Fuck Vera Knee."

"Good luck. She's gay." Arvin walks off, but not before favoring Charles with an oily smile.

Charles feels his mood curdle. He reaches for his wineglass and knocks it over, spilling its dregs on the white tablecloth. His stomach clenches and then burns.

Nina returns and sits down. "Charles, are you all right?"

"Fine. I spilled my wine."

"That means five years of good luck. It's an ancient African-American superstition I just made up." She signals for the check. "Back to the salt mines. We should hear about the paperback sale of *Capitol Offense* within the week. Should be three or four bidders."

"I should hope so," Charles says.

The waiter appears and as Nina signs the check, he slides the envelope across the table.

"What's this?" Nina asks, a glint of excitement in her eye.

"Just read it and give me your honest opinion."

"Have I ever given you anything but? Listen, Charles, I know *Capitol Offense* has been a rough haul, but hang in there. You'll prevail. You always have."

Charles walks Nina out and sees her into a cab. He stands on the sidewalk and realizes to his surprise that there's only one place in the world he wants to be at this moment: with Emma.

24

I T ' S A S P A R K L Y sort of New York evening, slightly breezy and cool, and Charles leaves the cab idling on Ninth Avenue while he and Emma dash first into a little market where he picks up an avocado, mushrooms, red pepper, onion, and garlic, and then to the deli next door where he grabs eggs, cheese, and a loaf of Italian bread. He looks casually handsome in his chinos and beat-up work shirt, and Emma loves watching him as he feels the avocado for ripeness, the pepper for firmness, asks how fresh the eggs are. He's insisted on coming to Emma's apartment to make the two of them his famous huevos rancheros for dinner. Anne is off giving a speech at a dinner celebrating women entrepreneurs.

The apartment is snug in the soft lamplight and warm neon underglow. Emma puts Brahms on her CD player and, his appointed sous-chef, she stands beside Charles as he peels the avocado.

"The avocado has to be so ripe it's almost melting," he says. "You can start chopping the onion and pepper. . . . I'd just moved to New York and was living in one room in Hell's Kitchen. *Life and Liberty* had been out for a month. I woke up one Sunday and it was number one on the *Times* best-seller list. Ten minutes later the phone rings. This five-pack-a-day voice says, 'Davis, this is Lillian Hellman and you're coming to my house for dinner tonight.' . . . No, no, tiny pieces, do a horizontal cut and then a vertical one.''

Charles demonstrates his chopping technique, their shoulders just barely touching. Emma feels cocooned, enfolded in a sweet lulling buzz, by his voice, his presence. She takes the knife from him and chops slowly, lovingly.

"That's it, Emma. . . . I get to her town house at eight o'clock. Hellman greets me. She's got this face so wrinkled it looks like a dried apple, and cigarette smoke pouring out of every orifice. She leads me into the living room—Mailer, Capote, not to mention Jane Fonda, Dustin Hoffman, and half of New York society. . . . The garlic has to be paper thin. . . . Hellman announces me and all these women wearing ten grand on each finger rush toward me. I felt like a headlight at a moth convention. . . . Thinner.''

"Thinner?'' Emma asks, her voice almost a whisper.

"The garlic has to be translucent; that's the great secret. . . . So I get cornered by a bleeding heart in an evening gown who's just read my book. She's carrying this special guilt about Vietnam because her husband inherited half of some chemical company that makes Napalm. I sprint off to the bathroom before I make a nasty scene, and bump into Olga, the six-foot Swedish maid, spraying an entire can of bug bomb into the toilet, nuking this poor water bug who doesn't know what hit him. . . . All right, I think everything's ready to go.''

Charles turns the burner on high, puts on a skillet, and pours in olive oil. He's so graceful, so deft, so at home in his skin, his *body*.

"Now every second counts. Dump in all the vegetables. Good. Sixty seconds and not one more. . . . After dinner, Mr. Napalm stands up and toasts me and all the boys who risked it all for the good old U.S. of A. He takes out a cigar, and Hellman, who's been chain-smoking through the whole meal, tells him cigars are verboten at the table. He sulks off somewhere, and some socialite starts rubbing my thigh. . . . Thirty seconds to go. . . . Mailer stands up to toast Hellman and everything is quiet when—*boom!*— there's this explosion like I haven't heard since the war. Olga comes running in, screaming 'The bug! The bug!' in her Swedish accent. Hellman slaps her across the face and everyone rushes into the hall. . . . The eggs." Emma pours the bowl of beaten eggs over the vegetables. "Two minutes here and thirty seconds under the broiler."

"Charles!"

"Turns out Mr. Napalm went into the bathroom to smoke his cigar, sat on the can, and tossed the match between his legs. The dinner party was shot . . . and so was his ass."

Emma laughs.

"Dammit, the cheese!" Charles cries. They both turn to reach for it and bump into each other. Emma freezes. Then she breaks away and pours them both more wine as Charles sprinkles the cheese on the eggs.

"So that, Emma, was my first night as a member of New York's literary elite. I hope yours is as much fun."

He looks at her. She turns away. Then she's in his arms and he's kissing her.

He begins by unbuttoning her shirt, slowly, gently, and she stands there and lets him, unsure what to do with her hands. How much can he tell by looking at her? She starts to tremble, and looks down, unable to meet his eyes. He puts a hand under her chin and raises her face, looking at her with his hazel eyes, his kind hazel eyes. They are kind, aren't they? Someone on the street below is honking his horn and shouting, "Come on, come on! Let's go!"

Come on, she hears. Let go, let go.

And then her shirt is off and he's touching her breasts, touching them lightly, kissing them. If only she could stop her body from trembling. If only that sign wasn't so bright, if only it was dark, and she could hide in the darkness.

Let go.

He unhooks her skirt and it falls to the floor. Is he trembling too? He kisses her while his hands slide down her back, and now she is naked.

Let go, let go.

But, no, she can't let go, she's afraid, it's too fast, she's naked, naked in front of him, and cold. She feels faint, wishes she would faint. But his hands are touching her, the small of her back and then her waist, her thighs. A shudder runs through her body, something she can't control. "Charles . . ." she begins.

But he puts his finger against her lips and leads her to the bed.

Charles stares down at Emma, at her naked body bathed in the crimson light. She's so pale, her face is shining, her eyes wide, those lovely haunted eyes. She keeps so much hidden. He wants to know her secrets, to possess her secrets. She looks so beautiful— does she know how beautiful she is?—and so afraid, this lost child. Then he knows: This is her first time.

It feels better, being on the bed, in the shadows. If only she could stop shivering. He puts his hand on her cheek, cradles her face, kisses her eyes, her cheek, her chin, leading her, so gently, forward.

"It's okay," he whispers.

Then he runs his fingers over her body, his touch so light, floating, touching her so gently. He runs his hand up her thigh, his strong hand, up her thigh, over her scars, and her breath catches, and his hand goes higher.

Let go.

With each touch she feels warmer, and his fingers play on her flesh, and his mouth is warm on her skin, and her flesh is moist under his fingers, and his body is strong and he's making love to her and, yes, she wants this, she wants him.

Charles knows it's time, she's ready, and he looks into her lost eyes, and he wants, needs, to be inside her. Poised between her legs, he wants her to look at him, at his body, to take pleasure from his body. And she does look, in wonder and confusion and want, and he enters her slowly, slowly, opening her up with his eyes. And then he stops.

Emma begins to cry. He kisses her and whispers, "Let go, Emma, let go."

And Emma does let go, arching her body, encircling him with her arms, her legs, pulling him in, closer, closer, until she doesn't know what she's doing anymore, doesn't care—feeling, for the first time in her life, a pleasure as deep as her pain.

25

EMMA ARRIVES AT WORK the next morning to find Anne Turner standing at the kitchen counter drinking a glass of grapefruit juice.

"Hello, Emma."

". . . Good morning."

"Is it?"

"Is it?"

"A good morning."

"I guess so."

"Outside, I mean," Anne says.

Emma can't look at her, can't answer, wonders what the rich bitch is doing in the kitchen. It's late; Emma has come in late on purpose, just to lessen the possibility of this very thing happening. Calm down, breathe easy, don't gulp air.

Dumb cunt, I fucked your husband.

"Oh. It's chilly out."

Emma knows it will look suspicious if she rushes off too

quickly. She has to look and sound natural, as if this is just another day. She tries to muster a smile, but it feels more like a tic.

"I love cold weather," Anne says.

"I do too."

"Do you?"

Anne is staring at Emma.

"How did your speech go?" Emma asks, grateful that she's thought of the question. She puts a hand up on the counter and tilts her head, hoping the gesture makes her look relaxed, interested, *normal*.

"Sisterhood is powerful," Anne says with a little smile.

What does that mean? Why did she say "sisterhood"? And that little self-satisfied smile—Emma wants to slap it right off her face. To just keep slapping until she kills the bitch. Slaps her dead.

"Sisterhood?" Emma asks.

"We women have to stick together. We can't start behaving like men."

"No, we can't," Emma says vehemently, shaking her head. How does Anne manage to look so good? She always looks good. Suddenly Emma feels dowdy and hopeless. And afraid. She shouldn't be here. She's making a terrible mistake.

BadGirlSickGirl.

"Charles and I are a little late getting started this morning," Anne says.

"Oh, he's not . . . ?" Emma gestures toward the office.

Anne shakes her head. "He's still in bed," she says with a wifely, proprietary grin.

"Excuse me," Emma says, needing to get away from Anne, away to the safety of her office, her work, Charles. No—Charles offers no safety. What a fool she was to think so. She moves toward the hallway that leads to the offices.

"Emma?"

Emma turns.

"Do you enjoy working for my husband?"

Emma feels herself start to sweat. "It's an interesting job."

"He's an interesting man." Anne reaches into a cabinet and takes out a bottle of vitamins. She shakes one into her palm and washes it down with juice. "His work seems to be going well. Does he discuss it with you?"

"No. Just a word now and then." Emma fidgets with the hem of her jacket and feels a pounding behind her eyes.

"And do you have aspirations?"

She can't tell her about her book, about Charles helping her, about the two of them working together. Emma tries desperately to think, to think what to say.

"Are you all right, Emma?"

"Fine. I . . . I want to go back to school. I think I'd like to teach."

"Charles used to teach."

"I didn't know that."

"He hated it."

Emma's headache is making her dizzy; her eyes feel like hot grapes. She closes them for a moment. Then she gestures toward the office. "I better get to work."

"You and me both," Anne says with a warm smile. "Have a good one." She turns and goes, leaving a hint of perfume in the air, something floral, exhilarating, and very expensive.

Emma stands there for a moment, at the edge of the vast white kitchen, stark morning light pouring in the window. The whole gleaming room seems to be mocking her: *Got too big for your britches, didn't you, dumbshit?* The cold rich room knows who she really is—how sick and sad and hopeless she really is—and it wants no part of her kind.

Emma turns and rushes down the long hallway. She collapses against her desk and tries to calm herself. Her head feels as if it's about to explode. She reaches into her bag for her bottle of aspirin, shakes out four, and swallows them down. She rolls up her sleeve quickly quickly, lights a match and watches it burn for several seconds before blowing out the flame and pressing the glowing ember against the smooth white flesh of her inner arm. The headache the pain the panic subside for a merciful moment. Suddenly the rug, the thick Persian rug filled with soft warm tones, looks so comforting, and Emma sinks down to the floor and lies on her side.

Charles closes his eyes and lets the hot water beat down on his face. His body aches a little, in a nice way. He feels his familiar masculine pride. He thinks of last night, of how he lost himself, of how long it has been since he's lost himself. Emma. Lovely, mysterious Emma. His need to understand her is becoming almost obsessive. And to protect her. Charles turns the faucet to cold, ice cold—he's even back to ending with a cold rinse, a long-abandoned ritual of his twenties. He feels his skin tighten, his brain sharpen, under the frigid assault.

Emma is sitting at her desk, so absorbed in her writing that she doesn't look up. He walks behind her chair and puts his hands on her shoulders. He feels her stiffen.

"Please don't," she says.

Oh, here it comes, Charles thinks: the second-thoughts syndrome. He bends down and kisses her neck. She bolts out of her chair.

"I made a mistake last night," she says.

He's taken aback—she's fierce, standing there clenching and unclenching her fists.

"I'm sorry you feel that way. It didn't look like a mistake to me," he says with a slight smile.

Emma is not amused.

"And I don't plan to make it again," she says.

"Emma . . ."

"Please don't patronize me. I'm here to work. That's where it begins and that's where it ends."

"Did you run into Anne?"

Emma doesn't answer.

"I'm so sorry, Emma."

"So am I."

"Can't we just step back and take a look at the situation?" he says.

"The situation is that you're a married man *and* my employer. That's two strikes, and I . . . I can't . . ."

Emma chokes and Charles moves toward her. The phone rings in his office. He ignores it, looking at Emma. She stands there, rubbing her hands on her thighs, not looking at him, struggling to hold her ground.

The phone rings again.

"Fair enough, but let's keep talking," Charles says.

He goes into his office, sits at his desk, and picks up the phone. "Yes?"

"Charles, right to the point," Nina begins. "Good news and bad. The bad is that we only got thirty thousand for the paperback of *Capitol Offense.*"

"Thirty thousand?!"

"It was the only bid. It's a blow, yes, but fuck 'em, you're still the best writer this country has produced in the last twenty-five years and no one's going to doubt it once they read this new work."

"What do you mean?"

"It's so right, going back to your small-town roots, writing from a young boy's point of view. And the mother—she's extraordinary! And terrifying."

"Nina, just a minute—"

"Don't be furious, but I've shown it to a few people, a few select people." Through the open door, Charles sees Emma get a drink of water, take a few deep breaths. "I hope you're writing. Don't let me interrupt. You're on to something, Charles. I have a *very* good feeling about this book. My love to Anne."

Charles slowly hangs up the phone, feels his chest hollow out, the room reel. Nobody wants his book, nobody wants it. He lets out a sound that's somewhere between a whimper and a moan. Emma appears in the doorway.

"Charles, are you all right?"

Staring down at nothing, Charles says, "I just got the lowest paperback sale of my career. One-tenth of what I got for my last book."

"I'm so sorry," Emma says. She takes a step toward him.

Charles stands up. He doesn't want to look at her; he needs air, needs to move, needs to be alone. "Not as sorry as I am." He walks past Emma, into the outer office. He hates her being there to witness his humiliation, hates the praise Nina gave her work. "By the way, Nina read your chapter," he says over his shoulder.

"You showed it to her?"

As he heads into the hallway, away from his shame, away from her, he turns. She has an idiotic expression on her face—apologetic hope. He hates pity. "She thought it had promise. I think you should finish the book and we can go over the whole thing before I send her any more."

"Whatever you say."

Christ, he hopes she isn't turning into just another suck-ass supplicant. Then she smooths her clothes in that awkward way of hers.

"You're going to be very famous," he says over his shoulder as he walks down the hall.

Manhattan can be the loneliest place in the world. Charles walks slowly, as he's been walking for hours now, in counterpoint to the city's rhythm, alone and out of step. He's free-falling down a black hole. How humiliating it will be when he tells Nina that he didn't write the chapter. How pathetic he'll look. He hates Nina for loving Emma's work, hates Emma for writing it, hates himself for hating them. As he walks the city's grid, his spiral of recrimination makes him dizzy, nauseated.

Finally the day begins to wane, bringing with it the comfort of late afternoon light, a softening of hard edges. Charles finds himself in Midtown, on Fifth Avenue, nearing Rockefeller Center. In his early years in New York, as success piled on success, this Art Deco kingdom was his favorite place. The statues and murals and fountains, the human scale and the soaring spirit—Charles saw it all as a metaphor for his work, as if his vision had been captured in light and water and stone. He would spend hours sitting beside the fountain, watching the people, mesmerized by the passing parade and the play of sunlight on granite and glass, knowing, on some level, that, like Fitzgerald, he was savoring a fleeting moment of grace, of simultaneous celebration and mourning.

Charles looks down the walkway that leads from Fifth Avenue to the skating rink. It's filled with laughing people, tourists in bright clothes, gawking at the fountains and the flowers, noisy, stuffing their faces with pretzels and ice cream. The world is so full of stupid people, bovine gimme-gimme people who don't know literature from lunch meat. One chortling man in a canary-yellow sweater and a cowboy hat is passing out hand-held video games to his three TV-addled, toy-mad midgets, while his beaming wife can barely stand up under her load of FAO Schwarz bags.

Charles turns and walks away from the mindless, squawking masses and finds himself staring into a bookstore window—a window littered with new books by blacks and gays and rich girls and poor people and lesbians and the diseased and the disfigured, all of them wallowing, wailing in second-rate prose their memoirs or barely veiled autobiographical tales of abuse, addiction, incest, struggle, recovery, and of course, insight and reve-fucking-lation. Or if they don't turn out sloppy sob fests, the women, quavering with pathos in their jacket photos, write from the womb in exquisitely measured sentences that read as if they've been strained through a sieve, so full of sensitivity and pain and crystallized moments that the goddamn books should be sold with a shrink-wrapped estrogen patch. The publishing industry isn't about great writing anymore, it's all about selling identity—race, gender, affliction, whatever pity party is drawing the biggest crowd this year. What a crock of self-indulgent shit it all is.

Next year Emma's book will be in this window. And where will he be?

26

ANNE IS IN THE FOYER about to leave for work. She stops
and listens. The apartment is quiet. Charles is in his office. It's a
warm morning, too warm for October, with that awful New York
humidity that makes your skin feel clammy. She ducks into the
study, closes the door, and picks up the phone.

When the women's health center answers, Anne lowers her
voice. "Yes, this is Kathleen Brody. I'm calling to see if my test
results are in."

"Please hold."

Anne stands absolutely still. A heavy bead of sweat rolls down
from her left armpit.

"Mrs. Brody?" It's Dr. Halpern.

"Yes."

"I tried to call you last evening. The number you gave us is
incorrect."

"Were you calling with my results?"

"I was. The blood sample you gave us doesn't match the DNA from your embryo's chorion."

"Thank you, Doctor."

Anne hangs up. She feels cold, as if her spine has turned to ice. And enraged. She dials again.

"Yeah?" The voice is groggy with sleep.

"Kayla, I'm sorry to wake you up, but . . ."

"Anne, what is it?"

"Charles isn't the father."

"Tell me this is a nightmare."

"What am I going to do?"

"You know your choices."

"It's my child, Kayla."

"Not yet, it isn't."

"Has Hollywood turned you into some kind of heartless monster? It's my child!"

Anne hangs up on her best friend. She opens the study door just in time to see Emma hurrying away toward the kitchen. The little toad had been standing outside the door listening. Maybe she's being paranoid—Emma might just have arrived for work. But she doesn't have her bag.

Anne rushes into the kitchen. Emma is halfway down the hall that leads to Charles's offices.

"Emma?" Anne calls.

Emma turns. She has an apple in her hand. "Yes?"

Anne waits as Emma walks back into the kitchen.

"Are you just arriving for work?"

"No. I was just getting a piece of fruit. I hope that's all right." She can't even look Anne in the eye.

"Help yourself."

Emma holds the apple with both hands and looks down. "Thank you," she says in that phony meek-little-girl voice of hers.

"You're among friends," Anne says.

"You've both been very nice to me."

"Well, you do a very good job. You're wonderfully efficient. And cooperative. That's very important for people like Charles and me. I'm sure you understand that."

Emma looks up and meets Anne's gaze. "Of course," she says. "Good."

Anne picks up a sponge and wipes away dirt that isn't there. She rinses the sponge and replaces it by the sink. She dries her hands on a dish towel.

"You know, I'm about to go through my closets—a little fall sweep-out. There might be some things that would fit you."

"You wear such beautiful clothes."

"I'm sure there'll be some things you'll like."

"Thank you."

Anne takes an apple from the bowl, looks at it, and then puts it back. "Well, I hope you and Charles have a productive day."

"Likewise."

Emma walks down to her office and pours herself a cup of coffee. The fact is, she *had* just arrived for work. She was stopped by Anne's voice coming from the study. She crept close to the door and listened. Except for "heartless monster," she couldn't make out the words—just the tone. Sounded like a fight with a lover. When she heard Anne hang up, she rushed into the kitchen, tossed her bag in the broom closet, and quickly grabbed the apple.

Emma sips her coffee with satisfaction. So rich bitch is having a little fling of her own. That changes everything. What's right for the goose is right for Emma.

Emma turns to the stack of papers on her desk, her previous day's output, gone over and carefully edited by Charles. He seems to understand Zack, the boy, and Sally, his mother, almost better than Emma herself does. He knows just how to change a word here, a description there, to make a scene come alive.

"Good morning."

Emma looks up. Charles is leaning against the old oak filing cabinet, wearing his faded work shirt open at the collar. He looks forlorn, and especially handsome.

"Good morning, Charles. You don't look like you got much sleep."

"I was working on your pages."

"Thank you. You know, Charles, I'm worried . . ." she says, and then lets her voice trail off.

"Worried?"

She nods. "I'm worried you've been neglecting your writing, paying too much attention to mine."

"I'm a big boy, Emma. You let me worry about my work."

"So you have been working on a new book?"

"No, it's an epic poem."

"Please don't be sarcastic, Charles. I'm just—"

He slams his fist on the filing cabinet and a stack of books on its edge crashes to the floor. He doesn't look sad anymore, but angry, a strange miserable anger that contorts his features. "Goddammit, Emma! Don't you think I know how to pace myself? Don't you think I've been doing this long enough to know when to sprint and when to hang back for a lap? Do I look like a rank amateur to you?"

"I only meant—"

"You only meant what? What? Spit it out, girl, you'll be a bigger man for it!"

"Please . . ." she gets out.

"Please what?" he hisses in a voice dripping with condescension and contempt.

"Please don't treat me like this." She stands and takes a step backward.

"Why not, Emma?"

"I can't— I can't take it. I'm sorry. I was just worried about you. Your work."

"You're not worried, Emma." He starts to come toward her, those bitter eyes staring her down.

"I'm afraid of you, Charles." She turns away from him, away from his rage. "I'm afraid of you."

"That's not really it, Emma, is it? Is it?"

And he takes her by the arms and spins her around. His hands are squeezing her hard, and she can smell his breath, clean and bitter, and his pine soap, and then she doesn't care anymore, doesn't care if he knows.

"No," she says. "No, no."

"Tell me!" he whispers.

And then the words pour out, acrid and defiant. "I love you," she says. "I love you."

Charles pulls her hair back and looks into her eyes. All the rage drains from his face and his eyes fill with longing. He leans down and kisses her, presses his body against hers.

Emma holds on to Charles, holds on as tight as she can, pulling him down with her, or lifting herself up, she isn't sure which. Does it matter anymore?

Later, at the end of the day, Charles goes out for a walk and Emma is alone in the office. She lies down on the floor and smokes a cigarette, feeling both exhausted and exhilarated. It's been a good day. She gets up, puts her coat on, and gathers up her day's work. She walks into Charles's office and puts the pages on his desk. Where is his work? She looks through the haphazard collection of papers on his desk: pages and pages of notes about her book, a phone bill, a take-out menu from a nearby Thai restaurant. That's it. She starts to open his desk drawers, searching for the spiral notebooks he uses for his early drafts. In the bottom left drawer she finds a pile of them and she lifts the top one out. She flips through it. The pages are blank. She takes out another and then another and then the last one. They're all blank.

27

"SPRINKLE ON THE CILANTRO at the absolute last second before you bring it out to the table," Anne says, standing over the pot of potato soup. The caterers are two young women with scrubbed faces. They come recommended, but she's never used them before. She dictated the menu, but didn't get home until the absolute last second herself, barely had time to change and greet her guests, and she has to take it on faith that they've followed her instructions. Anne hates to take things on faith. Especially lately.

"Where are the limes?"

The two young women look at her with blank expressions.

"The limes? To squeeze on the sorbet?" Anne says.

"You never mentioned limes," one says.

Anne sighs in exasperation. Of course she mentioned limes. She curses that idiotic photographer who took three hours to set up the afternoon's breakfast-in-bed shoot, throwing her whole schedule out of whack. She could have sworn she smelled pot on him. Anne reaches into the cabinet and breaks off half a peanut butter cookie.

"I didn't mention fresh limes to squeeze on the lime sorbet?" Anne remembers reading that Martha Graham swept the stage herself before every performance. Smart woman.

One of the caterers hands her a piece of paper.

"What's this?" Anne asks in a tight voice.

"Your fax."

Anne scans down the page to dessert: lime sorbet with ginger wafers. No mention of fresh limes. "You're absolutely right. Apologies." She runs her tongue over her back teeth; she's been grinding them again, in her sleep. "There's a deli on the corner. You'll have plenty of time to run down and buy limes after the soup is served."

Anne turns suddenly, sensing something behind her. The doorway leading to Charles's offices is open.

"Was that door open before?" she asks.

The caterers look at each other and shrug. "I didn't notice," one says.

"You haven't seen anyone go in or out?"

"No."

Anne steps into the hallway—down at the end the offices are dark.

"Is anyone down there?" she calls.

No answer. She closes the door.

"Is there anything I can do to help?"

Anne turns to see Nina standing in the kitchen doorway, cradling a glass of wine.

"I think everything's under control," Anne says, reaching for her own glass of wine and taking a sip. "How are you?"

"*Plus ça change* . . ." Nina says. "And you?"

"Hanging in."

"That's quite a tony crowd you've got out there. They're all new to me."

It's true, everyone at the party except Nina is a friend of

Anne's. In the early years of their marriage, Charles was the draw. Anne puts a hand on Nina's arm and discreetly leads her over to the far corner of the kitchen. Lowering her voice, she says, "I'm worried about Charles."

Nina is silent for a moment. She takes another sip of wine.

"He's taking the paperback sale very hard," Nina says finally.

"Kill the messenger?"

Nina nods ruefully. "It's difficult. We all know how much is riding on his next book." Anne feels a tingle of foreboding at the back of her neck. Nina sets her wineglass on the counter and leans in to Anne. "He gave me a chapter and it's sensational. But I can't get him to send any more or even to discuss it with me."

"But doesn't he always do that? Clam up? He's superstitious, afraid the energy will dissipate if he discusses a project."

"That's true. But he usually can't resist teasing me, giving me small samples, at least calling me now and then to rant and rave. Lately—nothing."

Anne wishes she wasn't having a dinner party, wishes she didn't have to be charming, didn't have to oversee the food, could just sit down with Nina and talk. She needs to talk. She drains her glass of wine and immediately wants a second but doesn't have it. "You know, there's this secretary, this temp I hired to help him get his office shaped up. I think I made a real error in judgment about her. She's strange, almost creepy, and I think untrustworthy. Of course Charles claims she's good for him."

Nina narrows her eyes and gives Anne a probing look.

"Believe me, I've considered that possibility. But it's hard to imagine Charles being attracted to her. She's all elbows and flusters—she can hardly complete her sentences." Anne hopes she sounds more convinced than she is.

Nina takes one of Anne's hands in both of her own. "Charles adores you, Anne, has from the moment he laid eyes on you. But right now I think he feels he's let you down, what with the disappointment of *Capitol Offense*. The old dog is as proud as a lion, you know. And he's at that age when men panic, that whole male menopause thing. I think what both you and I should do is give him some room for a little while. This new book is brilliant. I predict that a year from now we'll be laughing about this conversation."

Anne smiles and gives Nina's hand a squeeze. "What would we do without you?"

"You two are very important to me."

Anne glances over to see the caterers ladling out the soup. "Will you excuse me? I'll be out in two minutes."

Anne, determined to make the dinner a success, walks into the living room, her eyes doing a quick sweep of the sparkling room and its seven sparkling inhabitants. The president of a home shopping network sits on one end of the maroon Chesterfield—he's offered Anne the sun, the moon, and two hours of prime time to sell whatever she wants; that witty young screenwriter—she was an Oscar nominee this year— sits at the other end. Nina is lounging elegantly in an armchair; the husband-and-wife team of cultural arbiters who seem to turn out a book every year elucidating the state of America's collective psyche are sitting, tellingly, at opposite ends of the room; and standing by the window is the restless young heiress and socialite, according to *Fortune* the twelfth richest woman in the country, who is Anne's newest groupie and, she suspects, closet crush-holder.

Charles is holding forth by the fireplace, in high spirits, thank God. She knows he needs this social contact, this chance to shine. Dinner parties are one of the linchpins of their marriage and, in spite of Charles's recent railings against them, she knows how good they are for his ego—not to mention hers. At these parties they're a team again, an unbeatable team, two talented, generous people who are madly in love.

"The end absolutely justifies the means. What matters is the final work of art, not what it took to create it," Charles says, his hair falling boyishly over his forehead, his voice passionate.

Nina sits up and leans forward. "Oh, come on, Charles, that's absurd. Are you saying it would be all right to commit a murder so someone could write a great book about it?"

"If one sad, starving old peasant woman had to be murdered so that Dostoyevsky could write *Crime and Punishment*, so be it," Charles answers, raising a murmur around the room. Anne loves seeing him like this, in his element, the center of attention, tossing off ideas like shiny pebbles.

The female half of the cultural-critic team stiffens and says, "You're placing the artist on a different moral and ethical plane than the rest of humanity."

Charles is not deterred. "What would life be like without Mozart, Michelangelo, Shakespeare? What separates man from beasts? Art. It elevates us, illuminates our souls. Whatever the artist has to do to create is allowable."

Anne sees her opening and leaps in. "One thing we can all agree on: you can't create on an empty stomach."

The soup is a smash, of the earth, earthy, yet "somehow Parisian," the socialite announces. Charles and Anne sit at opposite ends of the table. The screenwriter, who is at Anne's left, has twinkly eyes that make Anne wonder if on her last trip to the loo she powdered her nose with something that packed a little more kick than talc. "What do you think, Anne?" she asks with a mischievous grin. "How would you feel if Charles were having an affair and justifying it by saying he was working on a book about adultery?"

"That would depend on whether or not I thought it was a great book."

"Let's assume it is," says the home shopping honcho.

"In that case, I'd expect him to be discreet enough to let me pretend I didn't know what was going on." Anne and Charles lock eyes as she speaks, both of them smiling tightly.

"But according to Charles's theory, he'd have every right to flaunt his affair," the honcho presses.

"Announce it over dessert," the annoying screenwriter adds.

"Well, this is only the soup course. But don't keep us in suspense, darling. Do you have any announcements?"

All heads turn to Charles. He slowly takes a sip of wine.

"I have two announcements," he says in a measured tone. The table grows silent. "First, I believe I am working on a great book. . . . And, second, it isn't about adultery."

Amid the general laughter, Anne is sure no one notices how forced hers is.

After the guests have left, Anne supervises the cleanup and then runs herself a hot bath and soaks for ten minutes. She assumes Charles is in his office, working. She puts on her nightgown and goes to say good night. She walks down the hallway and through the living room and dining room, turning off lights as she goes. The large apartment seems to grow cavernous in the dark. She crosses the kitchen and walks down the long hall that leads to his offices. They're dark.

"Charles?" she says tentatively, standing in the doorway of the outer office. There's no answer. She turns on the light and looks around the room, the room where Emma works. She goes over to her desk. It's neat and ordered, with a pile of letters, a list of things to do, a glass filled with pens and pencils. There's no idiosyncratic trinket, no picture, no struggling plant, not even a coffee mug. Anne slides open the top drawer. There's a box of Marlboros, a worn paperback copy of *Heart of Darkness*, a pack of chewing gum, paper clips, rubber bands. Anne sees the corner of a newspaper clipping that has been pushed to the back of the drawer.

She reaches in and lifts it out. It's a photo of her and Charles, taken at the library's Literary Lions dinner. There's an *X* scrawled across Anne's face.

Her heart pounding, Anne quickly replaces the clipping, closes the drawer, and leaves the room.

"Charles?" she calls from the foyer. There's no answer, yet she feels his presence in the apartment. She walks down the hall and checks the guest bedroom. Empty. Then she looks into the study. All the lights are off, but as her eyes grow accustomed to the dark, she makes out a figure lying on the couch. "Charles?"

"Don't," he answers.

"Don't what?"

"Turn on the light."

Anne suddenly wishes she'd put on her slippers; her feet are cold on the wood floor. She takes a cautious step onto the edge of the carpet. It's a moonless night.

"I just wanted to say good night," she says.

There is a long silence before Charles says, "It was a nice dinner. Thank you."

"Did you like everyone?"

"Sure. Swell crowd."

"You're mad at Nina, aren't you?" Anne waits for an answer, and when she doesn't get one, she adds, "You barely said three words to her all evening."

"Anne, she should have seen the paperback sale coming. She should have had a strategy."

"I agree it was disappointing, darling, but—"

"It wasn't disappointing, it was a disaster."

"Charles, I'm sure Nina—"

"It's always a mistake to mix business with friendship."

"Well, isn't that what you're doing with that secretary?"

Charles sits up, turns on a lamp, and leans forward with his elbows on his knees. "For Christ's sake, Anne, don't bring that up."

"I have a right to know what's going on between the two of you."

"What's going on is that I find, for some strange reason, that having her around is good for my work right now. When that ceases to be the case, she'll be gone."

"I don't like having her in the house. I think she's dishonest."

"That's ridiculous."

"Are you sleeping with her?"

Charles gets up and crosses to Anne, puts his hands on her shoulders. "You're kidding, of course." When she doesn't answer but just keeps looking at him, he adds, "No, I'm not sleeping with her."

Anne almost believes him. She suddenly feels terribly sad.

"I think I'm pregnant."

Charles drops his hands. "You're not sure?"

"No, Charles, I'm not sure."

"Well, then. When will you find out?"

"Are you happy?"

"I will be. Of course. The timing is . . . it's fine. When will you know for sure?"

"I've been putting off finding out. Maybe the timing *is* wrong."

"I don't have to tell you how preoccupied I am."

"I'm cold."

"Let me close the window."

After he does, he comes back and kisses Anne on the forehead. "We've wanted a baby for so long, haven't we? It's wonderful news."

"I suppose I should find out."

"Yes, Anne, do that. Find out."

"We'll have to think of a name. Do you like Eliza? Or Luke?"

"Let's not get ahead of ourselves."

Charles walks Anne back to the bedroom, and she climbs into bed.

"Listen, I'm feeling restless. Would you mind if I went out for a walk?" he asks.

"Don't be long."

After he's gone, Anne turns out her bedside lamp and lies there in the dark.

28

C H A R L E S   A N D   E M M A stand at the bow of the Staten Island Ferry as it returns to Manhattan. Charles has always loved this boat ride. He finds that the salt air and the panorama of water and sky, bridges and boats, has a way of clearing his head, loosening up his thinking, giving him a fresh perspective on the problem at hand.

He's hoping it will have a similar effect on Emma. They're at a crucial point in her book: Zack is about to break down under his mother's abuse. Charles is making aggressive changes, often re-writing whole paragraphs. He knows he's driving her hard, but he also knows it's good for her. Just as Portia guided him, he has to guide Emma.

Charles knows what will happen if he tells Nina that Emma wrote the chapter, shows her more of the manuscript: she'll want to start selling the book, get a buzz going, haul Emma off to lunches with editors. Emma is simply too fragile to handle that kind of exposure. No, it's best if they remain closed in, working in secret, and then, when the book is truly as good as it can and will be, they'll emerge triumphant to the world. Just as he dedicated *Life and Liberty* to Portia, Emma will dedicate *The Sky Is Falling* to him. He'll be associated with her success, given credit for passing on the mantle to the next generation.

It's a chilly day and the sun keeps disappearing behind the clouds, darkening the waters around them. With the wind whipping her hair, Emma seems content. He leans his shoulder into hers and is pleased when she leans back.

"How many people do you think are making love in this city right now?" Charles asks.

"A small fraction of the number who wish they were," Emma answers with a wry smile.

They lean into each other a little more.

"Charles . . . ?"

"What?"

"Nothing."

"No, what is it?"

"Well, I was just thinking about . . . this is hard for me. Your wife."

"What about her?"

"Has she ever, you know, had an affair?"

Charles laughs. "I highly doubt it." Emma stares down at the churlish waters. "What makes you ask that question?"

Emma shrugs.

And then, from behind them, a woman's voice: "Emma?"

Charles and Emma turn to see a pregnant young woman walking across the deck with a young man, obviously her husband, in tow. Emma's expression darkens.

"Is that you, Emma?" the young woman asks. She has short dirty-blond hair and wears no makeup, has a kind face with large gray eyes.

"Sue?" Emma says with a nervous laugh.

.   .   .

Nick's pizza parlor was where kids hung out after school in Munsonville. Emma didn't have any close friends, but sometimes she'd sit around nursing a slice, because anything was better than going home. A lot of the other kids in Munsonville came from screwed-up families, but Emma's mother was the undisputed town freak. Everybody who's down needs someone lower, and Emma's situation evoked condescending pity from her peers. Sue Jenkins—her dad sold plumbing and heating supplies, and her mom ran a store-front dancing school—was one of the few kids who tried to befriend Emma. Sue was sweet, and her family respected creativity. One Christmas they sent over a box of homemade goodies to Emma and her mother. Sue was popular, and one afternoon she invited Emma to tag along with her crowd when they went to Nick's.

They were all sitting around laughing and flirting—even Emma was starting to feel like part of the gang—when Emma's mother walked in. It was an early spring day, mild and breezy, but Helen Bowles was pushing the season in her red short-shorts, high-heeled mules, loose Hawaiian shirt, floppy straw hat, and pink plastic heart-shaped shades that looked as if they belonged on a three-year-old; her mouth, thick with ruby lipstick, leaped from her powder-white face. Her wrists were heavy with the usual Bakelite bracelets. Everything got quiet and Emma slid down in her seat. Helen threw back her shoulders and with a lopsided pride sashayed up to the counter.

"I'd like a 7UP, please," she said in that weird voice she affected in public—Julie Andrews playing a film noir gun moll. Helen was major-league stoned.

She took her soda and walked over to the jukebox. The place stayed quiet as she fed in her quarters. Madonna began to sing "Like a Virgin," and Helen Bowles started to dance in the middle of the dingy pizza parlor. "Like a virgin / Touched for the very first time."

Helen's dancing grew more and more exaggerated and suggestive. Nick was leering from behind the counter. One of the boys let out a whoop and started to snap his fingers. Others joined in, egging her on. Helen was in her glory. Sue gave Emma a look of pained sympathy. Helen slowly unbuttoned her Hawaiian shirt and then whipped it open, flashing her tits. That was when Emma ran out of the place.

Sue studies Emma for a moment before asking, with a peculiar intensity and sincerity, "How are you?"

"I'm fine," Emma answers, a little too casually.

"You look great," Sue says.

"So do you."

"I look like a whale. You remember Cliff." Cliff, a stolid sort, puts a protective arm around his wife, and exchanges a nod with Emma.

Sue and Cliff stand there waiting to be introduced to Charles. Emma tugs at her coat, bites her lower lip.

"Oh, I'm sorry. This is Charles. Sue and I went to high school together."

"Hi. I just can't get over how different you look," Sue says.

Emma smiles, still biting her lip. "We're not kids anymore." She quickly changes the subject. "What are you doing in New York?"

"The tourist thing, while we still have a chance." She pats her stomach and smiles. "What about you?"

"I live here. I have a job. I'm—"

Charles jumps in. "Emma works for me, she's my very able assistant."

"You look familiar," Sue says.

"Charles Davis? The writer?" Emma says.

"Wow. I saw the miniseries *Kings and Clowns*. Didn't you write that?"

"I wrote the book it was based on."

"Cool," Cliff says.

"God, Emma," Sue says. "In Munsonville they'd—"

"I know. Charles has been great. He's helping me."

Charles takes Emma's arm and firmly leads her off. "Enjoy New York," he says.

"Good-bye, Emma. Take care," Sue calls after them.

After the ferry docks, Charles and Emma walk along the Battery Park promenade. It's late afternoon and the park is virtually empty. The clouds have crowded out the sun, turning the sky, the water, the world, gray—that singular Manhattan gray that seems to have tiny shards of reflective light scattered through it. They walk slowly, Emma absently nibbling on popcorn they bought at a little stand outside the ferry terminal.

"Were you close friends with that Sue?"

"No, not really."

"Family friend?"

"No, we were in the same class, that's all. She was nice, but we didn't really have anything in common."

"Did you have a lot of friends growing up?"

"What is this—Twenty Questions?"

A tugboat chugs by close to shore; its horn blasts.

"Emma?"

"Hmmm?"

"I don't think we should discuss the book with anyone."

Emma tosses a handful of popcorn to a squirrel and out of nowhere a blizzard of pigeons descends.

"Look, Charles, we have this whole park to ourselves, just us and the pigeons and squirrels."

"You see, Emma, there are a lot of pitfalls for a young artist."

"Are there, Charles?" Suddenly Emma runs ahead of him and jumps up on a bench. "I can't believe Sue married that lug. Now she's stuck in that town forever. And I got out! I got out!" Emma upends the rest of the popcorn, and is quickly surrounded by a sea of fluttering wings and bobbing tails.

As Charles approaches, Emma jumps down off the bench and puts her arm through his. "I really am a writer, aren't I?" she says, trying on the identity like an expensive coat, one she lusts after but thought she could never afford.

"I would say so. Listen, I really think it's crucial that we keep our work to ourselves for the time being. Talking about it diffuses the energy."

"Who do I have to talk about it with? I don't think my Chinese grocer has much of a literary bent, even if he could speak English. I suppose I could call the psychic hot line and ask them how the book is going to end."

"Emma, I'm serious. Will you promise me you won't discuss it with anyone?"

Emma smiles up at him. "Cross my heart and hope to die."

29

CHARLES DUCKS INTO the damp dark of the midtown tavern. It's eleven-thirty in the morning and the place is just gearing up for the lunch rush, waitresses getting their stations set up, the soft clink of glass and silverware, the comforting smell of simple food and decades of drinking. He orders a double Scotch and water. He needs a drink to steel himself for the job ahead. It's really quite simple: Nina has to go. The paperback sale was a joke. And she hasn't even sold the film rights. He needs a young agent, somebody hip, with a big L.A. presence. Someone who can make him a lot of money. Fast. And then there's Nina's gushing over Emma's primitive prose. It's damn good, sure—*he'd* been the first one to recognize that—but the way she goes on you'd think Emma was the second coming of Faulkner. The book is in much better shape now, thanks to him, but the last person he wants to give it to is some over-the-hill agent who would probably sell it for a fraction of its worth. Poor Nina.

The portly bartender comes out of the kitchen carrying a big plate of french fries, which he secretes under his bar, shoving two or three into his face at a time. Charles remembers a crazy mid-summer day about fifteen years ago when he and Nina had cabbed out to Coney Island to satisfy a mutual craving for hots dogs and fries. They'd stuffed themselves like pigs at Nathan's, giggling, celebratory, madly in love with each other's success. And then they rode the Cyclone, Charles with his arm protectively around Nina, wanting the world to think they were lovers. They'd walked along the Boardwalk for miles, for hours, as the long day gave way to dusk and dusk to night. They were partners, and it was forever.

Well, forever is for fairy tales. This is a New York story.

As the elevator soars silently to the thirty-ninth floor of Nina's office building, Charles sucks on his breath mint. He's even worn a suit, a dark gray suit, to signify the solemnity of the occasion. He steps off the elevator and into the offices of the Nina Bradley Literary Agency. Esther—efficient, unflappable Esther, who's worked for Nina since the early days—sits at the reception desk.

"Good morning, Mr. Davis."

"Esther. Is Nina in her office?"

"She is. Shall I tell her you're here?"

"I'll just head down."

Charles walks down the long, carpeted hallway, lined with publicity posters for books Nina represents, Charles's prominent among them, past offices where well-dressed agents are working the phones. Jeffrey, Nina's latest assistant, a stylish young man Charles assumes is gay, leaps up from his desk when he sees Charles approach.

"Mr. Davis. Good morning. Is Nina expecting you?"

"No."

Jeffrey picks up his phone. "Nina, Charles Davis is here. . . . Of course."

Jeffrey hangs up and leads Charles across the hall.

Nina's pale gray office is dominated by her Pollock, bought when he was still affordable. Every line cool and uncluttered, the room epitomizes a certain post–World War II vision of modernism, a Midtown soul mate of Philip Johnson's New Canaan glass house. Guess what, Nina, the world's moved on.

Nina rises from her desk and crosses to Charles, taking his hand in her own. He's always loved the feel of Nina's hands and in a rush of emotion he considers ditching his plan.

"Charles, what a surprise. Can Jeffrey get you a cup of coffee? Something to drink?"

Charles shakes his head and remains standing. Jeffrey disappears.

"Charles, I am on such a high about this new book. When will I get more? I want to send a chapter to the *New Yorker*."

How can she do that? How can she think some unformed, uneducated kid from the outskirts of nowhere is a better writer than Charles Davis?

"Nina, please. This isn't a courtesy call. . . . This is difficult."

Nina's face grows grave. She sits behind her desk and waits for him to continue.

"For the first two decades of my career, I couldn't have asked for a better agent, but the last two books have been a disappointment. I feel that you mishandled them."

"You call the quarter-million advance I got you on *Down for the Count* mishandled?"

"I'm not talking about money. I need a fresh start, a rebirth. A resurrection."

"You're leaving me."

"I'm leaving you."

Nina looks down at her desk. Charles knows there won't be any tears, any curses, a scene. Breaks like this are best accomplished quickly, cleanly. In the end, it's all about the work. When she looks up at him all her polish and poise and sophistication are gone.

"Just like that, after twenty-four years?" she asks.

Charles meets her gaze; he owes her that.

"I'm hoping we can remain friends," he says.

They look at each other for a long time, compatriots for whom things will never be the same. Nina runs her fingers lightly up the back of her neck and then, as if a switch has been flicked, her jaw tightens.

"I'll call you next time I need a golf partner." She stands, walks to the door, and opens it. "Let Jeffrey know what you want from your files."

Charles knows how difficult she could have made this, could still make it, and he's grateful.

"Good-bye, Nina."

As he walks down the long hallway he feels guilty and exhilarated in equal measure. By the time he reaches the lobby the exhilaration has overwhelmed the guilt. Firing Nina is just the sort of bold move he needs to make a new beginning. Look at the work he's been doing with Emma. Why, he's practically writing her book, and doing it with a fervor and imagination that surprises even him.

Charles grabs an apple off the kitchen counter and takes a bite. He strides into his office and stops cold: Portia is sitting across from Emma, wearing black and smoking a Pall Mall. She looks tired and tiny, but fierce nonetheless.

"Jesus Christ, Charles, I know I'm a wrinkled old bag, but I don't look *that* bad."

Charles struggles to regain his bearings; as far as he knows, Portia hasn't been to Manhattan for years. How jarring to see her here, in this apartment, in this room—with Emma.

"Portia . . ."

"Another of the old Dartmouth dinosaurs bought the farm, so I crawled out from under my rock to see the old bastard off."

"Emma, why don't you take a break, get some air."

Emma stands up and puts on her coat.

"Don't take any crap from this guy," Portia says.

Emma laughs. "I'll try not to."

Charles watches as Emma walks down the hallway.

"Why, I'd love a drink," Portia says, reaching for her cane. She follows Charles into his office and sits down with a sigh. He pours two shots of Scotch, fighting to control the slight trembling of his hands.

"Bright girl," Portia says after taking a healthy swallow.

Charles notes the twinkle in her eye. "Oh, you two had a chance to talk?"

"No, I was too shy."

Charles fidgets with a tiny iron sailor he uses as a paperweight. Even after all these years, Portia has the ability to reduce him to a rattled kid. She's too fucking honest, like a moral flashlight aimed into his soul's darkest corners. Charles is sure she can tell that he and Emma are sleeping together. What else can she tell?

"What did you discuss?"

"She was very tight-lipped. You have her well trained. She said how interesting it was to work for you, how much she was learning."

Charles looks down into his drink. A pigeon coos on the window ledge.

"What's her background?" Portia asks.

"She's from some kind of broken home. I can't get much out of her. Tight-lipped, as you say."

Portia polishes off her drink and holds out her glass for a refill. "How are you, Charles?"

Charles wonders if he should tell her about firing Nina. They never talk career, only the work itself. Why bother her? Why get into all that explaining?

"I'm taking your advice, trying to stay in the game."

"Good. When can I read something?"

"Why is everyone on me? You can all read it soon enough." Charles immediately regrets his outburst. He stands up and walks over to the bookcase that's filled with foreign language editions of his books. "This is the Japanese edition of *Down for the Count.* Some cover, huh? . . . Don't look at me like that, Portia."

"Like what?"

"Like I'm going crazy or something."

"Charles, you've never stooped to melodrama."

"I'm sorry. I've been working too hard. But it's good. I think I'm on to something."

Portia knocks back her drink and stands. "Well, that's what I came to hear. Now let me catch my plane out of this hellhole."

Charles holds Portia's arm as they wait for the doorman to hail a cab. He has rarely touched her before and he feels self-conscious; he can feel her small bones and can tell she doesn't like being held. They don't look at each other.

"Send me something soon, Charles. I need reasons to stick around."

"It's always good to see you," he says.

"What's left of me."

At that, Portia smiles up at Charles. No, she beams, her whole face lighting up, embracing the absurdity, the futility, of the human condition, and suddenly it's nearly thirty years ago and Charles is a young man sitting in a New England classroom being inspired by a lonely woman who burns with a ferocious passion for the written word.

"There's lots left, Portia, lots."

It must be the New York air pollution that's making tears well up in Portia's eyes. Mercifully, a cab pulls up. The doorman holds open the door and just as Portia is about to climb inside, she turns.

"And, Charles?"

"Yes?"

"Be nice to that girl."

"I'll try."

Through the rear window, Charles sees Portia defiantly light up a cigarette. Woe be to that driver if he asks her to put it out. Then the cab disappears into the New York traffic.

30

ANNE IS WALKING down Sixth Avenue toward Le Bernardin
to have lunch with her mother. It's a cool sunny day and the air is
deliciously dry. She's decided to have the baby. If Farnsworth is the
father, so be it. The child will still be hers. And if her marriage to
Charles falls apart she won't be alone. She'll have Eliza, or Luke.
She pulls her phone out of her purse.

"Kayla."

"Anne."

"I'm sorry I hung up on you."

"No big deal. What's up?"

"I'm going to have the baby."

"You're sure?"

"Absolutely."

"Anne, that's sensational."

"You're going to be a godmother."

"Whatever the hell that is."

"Think expensive presents, savings bonds, that kind of thing."

"I'm going to come to New York and throw you a huge garish shower. We'll invite all sorts of celebs, get lots of press. You can start a new catalog called *Kids at Home*."

"It's already being prototyped."

"It's a bitch being best friends with a genius."

"Don't I know it. I'm on my way to have lunch with Mom, tell her the news."

"Oh, God, she's going to be so thrilled her face-lifts will crack. Even rich right-wingers love grandchildren. Makes them feel almost human. How's Charles taking impending fatherhood?"

"Haven't told him yet. Tonight."

Anne walks into the cool confines of Le Bernardin. Suddenly she's famished, longing for something rich and slightly ghastly, like a baked stuffed lobster. The maître d' is expecting her and escorts her to the choice front table where her mother is sitting. There's a man sitting with her, his back to Anne.

"Darling, there you are!" Frances exclaims.

The man turns. It's John Farnsworth. Anne feels her mouth go dry, her stomach hollow out. She puts a hand on the back of a chair to steady herself.

"Anne, how splendid to see you," Farnsworth says, standing and bowing slightly, a gentleman of the old school.

The maître d' pulls out Anne's chair and she sits.

"Anne, you look pale."

"I'm fine, Mother. Hello, John."

"I'm on my way out, I just popped over to flirt with your mother," Farnsworth says. "Of course she's much too young for me."

Frances laughs at the cheap flattery. She looks exquisite in a Barbara Sinatra-ish kind of way, her skin tight and luminous, her golden hair sweeping down to frame her face. She's wearing a beige wool suit with pink velvet trim—a southern Californian's idea of autumn style. She lays a hand on one of Anne's.

"It's so good to see you. How are you? Busy as a mad bee, no doubt. My daughter the superstar."

A waiter appears. Anne would love a martini but orders herbal tea. Farnsworth orders Scotch, and Frances carrot juice spiked with a shot of vodka.

"My yoga teacher approves of vodka," she announces.

"We won't bore your mother with business talk, Anne."

"Oh, go ahead, my husband does it all the time," Frances says. She and Farnsworth laugh.

Anne has a hard time looking at him, at that jowly red face. She gets a whiff of his bay rum and it brings back a flood of memories—that bay rum curdling into sweat and lust and sour breath. She wants to pick up her knife and jab it into his eyeball.

"She's quite a gal, this daughter of yours," Farnsworth says. He places a moist heavy hand on one of Anne's. She pulls hers away and opens her napkin.

"I'm so proud of her. You know that, don't you, darling?"

"Thank you. I think I get a lot of my drive from you."

"And your beauty," Farnsworth adds.

"Isn't he awful?" Frances says to Anne.

"Awful."

Their drinks arrive. Anne inhales the soothing aroma of her chamomile tea.

"News flash—I snagged Jay Leno for our hospital benefit," Frances announces. "Terribly nice man. Absolute professional. We're going to raise two million or I'm a monkey's uncle."

"That's terrific, Mother."

"I probably should have gone into business myself. But back in *my* salad days, women just didn't."

"Oh, you wouldn't like business, Frances. You're far too cultured. Business is brutal. Isn't it, Anne?"

"It certainly can be."

"We cover it with a veneer of civility, but it's really the law of the jungle out there."

"Well, here's to the veneer," Frances says, lifting her drink and taking a long swallow. "God, I adore carrot juice."

Anne feels as if she's stepped outside herself and is watching the scene from a remove. The muffled clink of dinnerware and chatter of the other diners becomes a surreal buzz. Her limbs begin to tingle. She puts her hands around her teacup for warmth.

"Anne, has John told you that he and Marnie have endowed a gallery at the Museum of Fine Arts up in Boston? It's terribly exciting. The dedication ceremony is in March. Dwight and I are going," Frances says.

"How *is* your wife?" Anne asks.

"Marnie? She's fine. Up to her ears as usual."

"That's good news. Last time I saw you she was ill."

"Oh, that. Turned out to just be a forty-eight-hour flu."

Sour bile bubbles up at the back of Anne's throat. "Will you excuse me?" she says quickly. She stands and forces herself to take measured steps as she crosses the restaurant. In the ladies' room, she leans over the toilet and retches out a thin stream of watery brown fluid. She sits down and waits for the dizziness to pass. Her mouth tastes rancid. She hastily gets a cup of water, rinses out her mouth and spits into the sink, then takes a long drink. With her mouth open she draws deep, steadying breaths. Finally she feels halfway human. She pulls her phone out of her purse.

"Dr. Arnold's office."

"This is Anne Turner, may I speak to Dr. Arnold please, it's an emergency."

As she waits for the doctor to come on the line, Anne presses a palm against the cool marble of the sink.

"Judith Arnold, Anne."

"I'd like to schedule an abortion. As soon as possible."

"Are you all right?"

"I'm fine."

"You're sure?"

"Yes. I just want to get this over with."

"You're at approximately how many weeks?"

"Twelve."

"Then we don't have much time." There's a pause and then Dr. Arnold says, "How's Friday at eleven?"

"Good."

"See you then. You're sure you're all right?"

"I'll be a lot better after Friday."

When Anne returns to the table, Farnsworth is standing with his hands on the back of his chair.

"I'm off. It was a pleasure seeing you both. Anne, let's have lunch next week."

"I'll call you," Anne says.

"And, Frances, if you ever want to make a little mischief . . ."

"Oh, be gone, you terrible man," Frances says with a big smile.

Anne sits down and looks at her perfect little salad, which she can't possibly eat.

"I swear John Farnsworth and your stepfather are cloned from the same DNA," Frances says, taking a bite of her salad. "Superb salad. Anne, what *is* the matter with you? I know—Charles's book. Well, darling, that's what you get for marrying a man in the arts. Live by reviews, die by reviews. Now what's the big news you were going to tell me?"

Anne takes a drink of water.

"Oh, that. Just that the *Home* website is up. It looks great. Sales are strong."

"Why, of course they are. Oh, look, it's Sadie Post." An L.A. X-ray approaches the table in a shimmery white pants suit no self-respecting New Yorker would be caught dead in, even *before* Labor Day. "You naughty girl, you didn't tell me you were going to be in New York. You know my celebrity daughter, don't you?"

"Mother, I didn't realize how late it was. I'm not going to have time for lunch."

"Then you'll join us," Sadie says to Frances.

As she walks out into the reviving air Anne has only one thing on her mind—revenge. She takes her phone from her purse and calls Kayla.

31

AS CHARLES'S JAGUAR approaches the Newark Airport exit, Anne is taking a mental inventory of what she's packed for her overnight trip to Chicago: jogging shoes for her run by the lake, a suit for her tour of a South Side textile factory she's thinking of contracting, a dress for dinner, slacks and a shirt for the flight home. Usually these quick mental scans reassure her. Not this time.

Anne looks out the window at the airport approach road lined with squat, graceless buildings. Suddenly the world seems a bleak, senseless place. Dread sweeps over her. The day after tomorrow she'll have the abortion.

She looks over at Charles. The other night, in the middle of a conversation, he forgot what they were talking about. She reaches over and touches his forearm. "I hate to be going away right now."

"It's only overnight."

"Overnight can be a long time."

"Anne, don't worry," he says, not taking his eyes off the road.

"I can't help it."

"What about the pregnancy?"

"It may just be that stress has been throwing off my period. You know how that sometimes happens to me."

Charles pulls out a pack of cigarettes.

"Oh, shit, give me one," Anne says.

Charles hands her the pack and she lights one. He doesn't.

The cigarette tastes hot and acrid, but she keeps smoking it. "I don't understand why you fired Nina."

"Let's face it, Anne, she wasn't delivering."

"But she's a friend."

"I know she is. And I hope she can remain one."

"Would you mind if I called her?"

"I'd rather you didn't. Look, Anne, it wasn't easy for me. I think a fallow period would be best."

"I don't know if I can just let her go like that."

"For Christ's sake, Anne, the woman is losing her touch. And I'm not going to let friendship or anything else stand in my way."

There it is again, that tone in his voice, that harsh, heartbreaking tone. It scares Anne.

"Your work's going well, that's the most important thing," she says, almost to herself.

Charles pulls up in front of the terminal, they get out, and he retrieves Anne's bag from the trunk.

"You can still surprise me, Charles."

"I hope the trip is a success."

Anne throws her arms around his neck and kisses him, long and hard, not wanting to let go.

"I'll call you tonight," Charles says.

"I love you."

Anne picks up her bag and walks to the terminal doors. She turns and smiles at Charles. He smiles back and waves. She walks into the terminal and then turns for one last look. The car is gone.

.   .   .

As Charles pulls away from the terminal he reaches for his car phone and punches in Emma's number.

"Hello?"

"Listen, Emma, I've got some appointments today, let's take the day off. Don't bother coming in."

"But what will I do with myself?"

"I hope you'll write." Charles smiles—she's at a loss without him.

"Of course."

"I'll call you tonight. I'll try to make it down there so we can get a little work done."

Charles listens to Miles Davis as he drives across Pennsylvania, propelled by his need to understand Emma, to discover what it is in her past that she guards so warily. He looked up Munsonville in his atlas and there it sat, surrounded by other small towns, black dots connected by red lines on a green background. It was there, in that western Pennsylvania town, that her life—and their book— began, and he needs to see it in three dimensions, to smell it, hear it, feel it, to find Emma's place in it.

It's afternoon when he exits the turnpike. The countryside is bleak—low hills littered with mobile homes and sagging barns. As he approaches Munsonville, the scene grows bleaker still, the small houses close together, aluminum-sided, painted dreary shades of light green or dark brown; the children playing in the ratty front yards look ill-kept and furtive, suspicious of life already. In the center of town, the houses give way to nineteenth-century brick buildings. The only businesses that seem able to survive on the beat, forsaken streets are bars and pizza parlors. Some of the empty storefronts have droopy For Rent signs taped to their win- dows; others just sit there, hollow and abandoned. A very pregnant girl wearing a dirty Palm Springs sweatshirt slowly pushes a young boy in a stroller.

Charles finds the palpable air of decay evocative, almost romantic. He thinks of Emma walking these streets, wonders which house she grew up in, wonders where her mother lives. Emma said she'd remarried. What's the stepfather like?

Munsonville High is set on a rise just outside of town, an imposing American Gothic edifice built in a more optimistic time. The hallways have that deserted, slightly eerie after-school feeling. Charles walks past posters warning of HIV transmission and the dangers of cigarettes, past a cabinet filled with dusty trophies, until he comes to a frosted-glass door that reads: Guidance Office. He knocks.

"Come in."

The front room is empty, but a woman is sitting at a desk in one of the four small offices that open off it. She's reading something in a folder. A sign on her desk identifies her as Claire Eldredge.

"Ms. Eldredge?"

"Yes."

Charles guesses she's in her late fifties, large, one of those round-faced women who has probably looked the same since her mid-twenties. She wears her glasses on a chain, a loose gray dress, no makeup. Claire Eldredge's one vanity appears to be her hair, which is an unnatural brown, styled in a helmet of tight curls.

"I'm sorry to disturb you."

"I rarely leave before six. This job just keeps getting harder." She looks at Charles expectantly.

"My name is Charles Davis."

"The writer."

"Yes."

If Claire Eldredge is impressed, she does a good job of disguising it.

"Have a seat. What can I do for you?"

"One of your former students works for me. I've become a little concerned about her."

"What's the student's name?"

"Emma Bowles."

Claire Eldredge's face grows grave. She leans forward on her elbows.

"I believe she graduated five or six years ago," Charles says.

"Emma never graduated."

"She didn't?"

Claire Eldredge closes the folder on her desk and puts it aside. She takes a pencil out of a cup and turns it between her fingers.

"Emma was gifted, but I could never reach her. She was very much a loner."

"Can you tell me anything about her family?"

"The father ran off when Emma was very young. Helen Bowles wasn't the most stable person to begin with."

"Her mother?"

"Yes. She painted. Or did at one time. Went to art school in Chicago. Fancied herself a bohemian. Dressed outlandishly. Hated Munsonville and wasn't shy about letting people know it. They lived above the hardware store downtown. She drank. Pills, too. The household was chaotic. Emma did all the shopping, cooking. Not that there was much of either. Helen wouldn't let Emma have a life of her own. Personally, I think she hated her daughter for being bright and talented."

"She certainly is talented."

"More than once she came to school with bruises. She'd often start to cry for no reason. We did a couple of home visits, but Emma always defended her mother. Afterward everyone said they saw it coming."

"Saw what coming, Ms. Eldredge?" Charles asks too quickly.

Claire Eldredge looks him in the eye. "What exactly are your concerns, Mr. Davis?"

"Well, I'm not entirely sure. She seems so unhappy, so unstable. I want to know why."

"There's bound to be instability with a history like hers. I'm glad she's working for you. Give her my best."

"Ms. Eldredge?"

"I've said too much already. It's all in the past. Everyone deserves a second chance."

32

MUNSONVILLE'S BOXY ONE-STORY library is drafty and
ill lit, smells of floor wax, and has a meager array of current titles
displayed on a folding table. It's staffed by one distracted middle-
aged male librarian. Charles sits in a far corner staring at the screen
of a microfilm viewer, scrolling through front pages of the *Munsonville Daily Press*. Hyperalert, focused like radar, he scans past
stories of storms and car crashes—and then he stops:

MUNSONVILLE WOMAN BLUDGEONED TO DEATH
DAUGHTER CONFESSES TO CRIME

HELEN BOWLES, 36, of 12 West Bridge Street, was murdered
early Tuesday morning, according to Sergeant Rupert Markum of
the Washington County Sheriff's Department. At 3:14 A.M., a 911
operator received a call from the victim's daughter, Emma Bowles,
who stated, "I hurt my mother." Officers Ellen Grady and Karl

Werner responded to the call, and when they arrived at the scene they discovered Mrs. Bowles's body lying on the floor of her daughter's bedroom. The victim had received multiple blows to the skull from a blunt instrument. A small metal lamp found beside the body was covered with blood. According to Officer Grady, Emma Bowles was sitting on the floor near her mother's body and said, "I did it." Officer Grady described Miss Bowles, 15, as "weirdly calm." She was taken to Juvenile Hall at the Washington County Jail, where she is being held on $100,000 bail.

Accompanying the story is a photograph of Emma's bedroom. Helen Bowles's body is covered with a blood-soaked sheet. There's an old iron bed, a cardboard dresser with a goldfish bowl on top, unruly piles of books everywhere, and a poster of Edward Hicks's *The Peaceable Kingdom* on the wall. The walls are splattered with blood, sperm-shaped streaks, as if someone holding a sopping paintbrush had whirled around and around in the middle of the room.

Charles feels a sense of disbelief, as if the story and picture aren't real, exist only on the screen. He sits stock-still, suspended, his breathing shallow, the library silent. Finally he resumes scrolling.

DAUGHTER CLEARED OF MURDER CHARGE
Jury Rules Teen Not Guilty in Killing of Mother

A WASHINGTON COUNTY jury has found Emma Bowles, 15, not guilty by reason of insanity in the March 12 murder of her mother, Helen Bowles. The deciding factor, according to one member of the jury, was the testimony of a psychiatrist who examined Miss Bowles and reported that she was the victim of chronic abuse. A medical examination offered in evidence documented broken bones, contusions, and sexual trauma suffered by Miss Bowles at her mother's hands.

Accompanying this article is a photo of Emma, wearing a jail-issue smock, being led out of the county courthouse. She looks passive, tranquilized, her hair tangled, her eyes vacant.

"Closing time," the librarian calls to Charles.

"Five minutes," Charles says, his eyes avid on the screen as he scrolls forward, pulse pounding. The librarian lets out a weary theatrical sigh, which Charles ignores.

EMMA BOWLES ATTEMPTS SUICIDE

OFFICIALS AT Keystone State Psychiatric Hospital in Randall reported that Emma Bowles attempted suicide last night. She was discovered hanging from a ceiling pipe in the women's lavatory. Rushed to the infirmary, Miss Bowles was resuscitated and is now listed in fair condition.

Miss Bowles has been at Keystone State for seven months, since being found not guilty by reason of insanity in the murder of her mother. She was committed to the hospital by Judge Leo Holderman when found to be a danger to herself. Dr. Alton Waters, the head of the hospital's juvenile ward, stated, "The staff at Keystone is saddened by Emma's setback. She seemed to be making progress. However, she is consumed by guilt and recently complained of aural hallucinations. We may be seeing incipient schizophrenia."

As dusk descends, Charles walks down Main Street. The neon glow from the bars and pizza parlors softens the forlorn street. A little girl appears at the open door of one of the bars, looking around for someone to play with; a melancholy Country Western song drifts out from the jukebox.

Charles turns onto West Bridge Street, which has no comforting lights, just a row of vacant brick buildings that give way to scruffy fields and the sky beyond. He comes to number 12. Under the For Sale sign over the doorway, he can make out faded lettering: Oversby Hardware. The windows of the apartment above are blocked by yellow shades. Charles tries the door that leads up to the apartment—locked. He walks down the narrow alley that runs alongside the building. At the far end is a wooden staircase leading to the second floor.

Charles looks around: no one. He climbs the stairs. At the top is a door with a square of small windows in it. Again, locked. He tries to force it; it rattles but holds. He jabs his elbow through one of the windows; the glass shatters. Charles freezes, waiting. The faint wail of the jukebox is all he hears. He reaches in through the window and releases the lock.

Charles finds himself in a dark, dusty hallway. The building is too quiet, as if someone is hiding in it. At the end of the hallway is a door. He gives it a little push and it swings open.

Charles moves slowly into the apartment. Dim light struggles in through the cracked shades. He stands still while his eyes adjust. He takes out the pocket flashlight he keeps in his car and runs its beam over the scene. The living room is piled with crates, window screens, rakes—remnants of the dead hardware store. Water stains bloom on the floral wallpaper. He walks into the bathroom; the sink, tub, and toilet are dry and rust-stained. The linoleum is curled up at the corners, the air dense with dust motes.

Charles looks at himself in the medicine chest mirror. His face looks gray, sunken, cadaverous. He opens the medicine chest, its rusty insides hold the shriveled carcass of a bar of soap, one curled and crumbling Band-Aid, a rusted lilac powder tin—Lady Lovely. Charles twists the top, lines up the tiny holes, and shakes a little of the pallid powder into his hand. It smells stale and sickly floral, like something you'd put on an ancient stroke victim on her birthday.

Somewhere in the distance an ambulance speeds down a country road, its siren shrieking into the deaf, descending night. Charles walks down a short hallway and into Emma's bedroom. The old iron bed is still there, the faint bloodstains are still on the walls, the sadness is still in the air, the thick air, in the last gasp of twilight. Sitting in a corner is the empty goldfish bowl, thick with dust. Charles imagines Emma in this room, abused and alone.

"She killed her here."

Charles swings around and the flashlight's beam lands on a
woman standing in the doorway. For a second he thinks he's hallu-
cinating. She's somewhere just this side of old, bone-skinny, in
tight jeans pegged at the ankles and a sweatshirt pushed up at the
elbows. Her face is bloated and shiny—is it bruised?

"You got a cigarette?" Her voice is cagey, conspiratorial.

Charles stares at her for a long moment before handing her his
pack of Marlboros.

"Keep it," he says.

She shakes out a cigarette and searches for a match. Charles
hands her his book. She lights up and inhales deeply. "You're not
going to tell them I'm up here?"

"No," Charles says softly.

"No one'll rent it anyway. Bunch of superstitious yokels." She
gives Charles a wily, assessing head-to-toe, opens her mouth and
runs the tip of her tongue along her upper lip. Then she throws
him a pitying, dismissive look, turns, and walks out of the room.
Charles listens as her footfalls fade, swallowed up by the silence, by
the building, by the town.

Charles stops at the diner by the turnpike entrance and gets a cup
of coffee to go and a pack of cigarettes. He heads for the pay phone
back by the rest rooms and dials Emma's number. She answers on
the second ring.

"Emma? What are you doing?"

"Just going over your notes."

He imagines her in her nightgown, sitting up in bed, a pad
propped up on her knees.

"Good girl. Listen, I'm trapped in an incredibly dull dinner
meeting with some legal types. I'm not going to get down there
tonight. But I'll see you in the morning. And, Emma?"

"Yes?"

"I love you."

He hears her breath catch.

"I love you, Charles."

"I'll see you in the morning."

Charles hangs up the phone and walks out into the night.

33

EVERYTHING IS DIFFERENT today—the light through her window, the way it feels to cross the room. Emma washes her hair and leaves it down; she puts on a new black wool skirt and a cream linen blouse and a pair of black Italian flats for which she paid the unheard-of price of sixty dollars.

As she walks to the subway, Emma passes a woman rummaging through a trash can for returnable bottles. She's middle-aged and her clothes are dirty, but she has on a beret and the clunky black shoes popular with downtown hipsters. Emma stops and opens her purse to give the woman a dollar—on the bottom sits her little painted tin. She lifts out the tin and looks at it for a moment, before opening it, unfolding the velvet, taking out the razor blade, and dropping it down the storm drain.

"Would you like this?" she asks the woman.

"I'll take money too."

Emma laughs and gives the woman the tin and a dollar.

She arrives at work and is surprised to find Charles, in a bathrobe, sitting at the kitchen table. He's drinking a cup of coffee and reading pages from her manuscript. Without saying a word, he stands up and puts his hands on her shoulders and looks at her in a peculiar, probing way. She opens her mouth to say something and he puts a finger to her lips. Then he kisses her. Outside, the day is gray, the sky low, the city closed in, the apartment a world apart. She meets his kiss with her own.

Charles begins to unbutton her blouse and she reaches into his robe and feels his chest; the robe falls open, he has nothing on underneath, his muscular body is naked, and Emma wants to look at it, right there in the kitchen. She breaks their kiss and pushes the robe off his shoulders and he stands there in front of her, naked. Emma lets her eyes roam down his body. It's *her* turn. And maybe someday soon this will be *her* kitchen.

She feels Charles's hands on her shoulders, applying a growing pressure. Emma sinks to her knees and the room falls away.

"You're mine," he states.

Emma looks up at him, but he grips her hair and forces her gaze down, down.

"I'm yours," she whispers.

Their sweat and juices mingle until their bodies share the same dense smell. Emma steps through the looking glass into a realm of pure sex, moving openly, naked, from room to room, making love in the guest bedroom, on the rug in the library, until the day becomes a blur, a hazy blue high, a languid dream of love and desire. Now they're dancing naked in the shuttered living room to the music of Billie Holiday and Emma wishes her father could see her, could see how she's grown up into a woman, a woman who dances naked to Billie Holiday in the middle of a gray New York afternoon.

The day slips by like a vapor and Emma finds herself on the living room floor wrapped in the softest blanket she has ever felt, her body aching with the sweetest fatigue. Charles, wearing his robe, is sitting in the chaise longue reading to her from *The Sound and the Fury.*

Charles closes the book and looks down at her. Emma lets the blanket slip from her shoulders and she's naked in front of him on the floor. She leans back and opens up her body to him, an offering, and he looks and she loves his looking. Then she drapes her arm around his ankle and kisses his foot.

Charles is holding her down on the bed, gazing at her with something hard and frightening in his eyes. Emma pleads with her eyes; she needs him, needs him inside her. She starts to whimper, and still he just looks down at her.

"Please . . ." Emma moans.

A tiny smile plays at the corners of his mouth and he moves his hips closer so that he brushes against her, hard and hot.

"Please . . ."

And she arches her hips up and he moves out of her reach and her breath comes shallow and she knows if she can have him she will never want anything else.

"I beg you . . . Charles . . ."

"Say it," he orders quietly, staring down into her eyes.

"I beg you . . . please, Charles, I need it, I beg you I beg you I beg you . . ."

And then she starts thrashing on the bed, her body sweeping her up in its need. And he enters her, and feeling him, she stops and is still—and as he slides in, slowly, slowly, she remains still, biting her lower lip, looking into his eyes, knowing she has found that place where love lives.

When Emma wakes she's alone in the guest room, and outside the window it's dusk and she wonders where Charles is. The apartment is silent and empty, and suddenly she's scared, gripped by fear in the huge room with its empty corners. She sits up, sweating. What's she doing here? Naked. She's in danger. She must get out, get home—home. Where is her home? Panic rises in waves up her body.

And then she hears footfalls coming down the hall. She's still. Charles walks into the room, dressed, with his coat on, and he smiles at her. He switches on a bedside lamp and a soft amber glow suffuses the room. Her panic recedes, but it's quickly replaced by a terrible vulnerability, being naked on the bed, as if the party's over and no one has told her. And then Charles leans down and kisses her and she wraps her arms around his neck and everything is all right again. She has simply taken a nap, a nap after a long day of lovemaking. Grown-ups do that.

"Hungry?" Charles asks.

"Mmmmm." She realizes she's ravenous.

"Thai?"

Emma nods.

"Back in twenty minutes."

And then he's gone and Emma is alone in the apartment. She stretches. Her body feels heavy and warm and satisfied. She catches her reflection in the mirror over the dresser. Lit by the soft yellow light she looks almost beautiful, like an actress in a sexy French film, glamorous and languid, alone in her lover's apartment in the evening.

Emma has a sudden urge to explore, and she slips out of bed and into her shirt. She loves walking down the long hallway in nothing but her shirt—she *is* in a sophisticated French film.

Emma walks into the master bedroom and stops. The vast sleigh bed stands dead center in the room like a surly watchdog. Emma gives it the finger. Poor rich bitch, Charles has never taken her to the places he took Emma today, no way. On the dresser sits a tiny kingdom of beautiful glass bottles. Emma opens one and holds it under her nose—it smells fresh and clean and full of hope. She dips the stopper and runs it along her neck and down into her shirt, between her breasts, around a nipple.

In the bathroom Emma looks at herself in the mirror wall. Her skin is glowing, her face infused with a confidence she's never seen before. Slowly, defiantly, she begins to unbutton her shirt. It falls off her body and she stands there naked. She's never looked at herself like this before. She's a woman now and her body shows it: her bony, boyish angles have softened, her hips and breasts have filled out and, yes, they do have a lovely shape, graceful and smooth. She's a woman and a writer and she has a lover and a book—a life.

Emma steps into the shower, the huge shower with its brushed-steel bench and shelf filled with expensive soaps and shampoos, everything glistening, and she turns on the faucet and the water sprays out, steaming, soothing, and she lets it beat down on her body, her strong beautiful body.

Wrapped in a thick towel and drying her hair, Emma walks across the bedroom and into rich bitch's dressing room. It looks like a department store. One dress catches her eye, a plain black dress made of some material that seems to float as she takes it down. Emma turns to the full-length mirror, and holds the dress up in front of her. It has thin shoulder straps, and ends halfway down the thigh. It's such a simple dress, and yet the cut, the cloth, and the feel are sublime. Emma imagines wearing it out to dinner with Charles in the summer, sitting at an outdoor café, elegant and famous and in love, watching the city go by. She hangs up the black dress and takes down a pale green one, full-length, silk, elegant, tight, with a mandarin collar and a row of tiny buttons running diagonally across the chest. She turns to the mirror—how wonderful! Like something you'd wear to the White House or to an opening night, on Charles's arm, secure, serene, and beautiful.

"Green's not your color."

Emma gasps and whirls around. Anne Turner is standing in the doorway.

"I'm . . . I'm sorry. I don't know what I was doing."

Emma, her hands shaking, hangs the dress up and makes a move to leave. Anne blocks her way.

"The point is, Emma, I do know what you're doing."

Rich bitch has her face all haughty and righteous. As if she were so perfect.

"You said you were going to give me some of your clothes, didn't you? Remember—a few weeks ago, in the kitchen? Right after that phone call?"

Anne is stunned. Emma thinks she looks like a fucking cow, standing there with her mouth gaping open.

"Well, didn't you?"

Anne takes a step backward. "I didn't think you'd come and help yourself," she says crisply.

"I'm just checking them out," Emma says. She turns and runs a hand along the dresses.

"Anne, you're home," Charles says, walking into the room, shooting Emma a glance that says "I'll handle this."

"I'm home."

"I thought your flight got in at midnight."

Anne purses her lips and spits out, "We had favorable tailwinds."

"I told Emma she could take a shower."

"Did you also tell her to slip into something comfortable while she was at it?"

"Emma, the food is up front. I'll be right there."

Anne is alone with the bastard and there isn't a lot of room to maneuver in the small space.

"Does she fuck as well as she types?"

"Don't be vulgar, Anne."

"You're screwing your secretary in our apartment and you accuse me of being vulgar?"

Charles lowers his voice. "Anne, there's something about Emma I haven't told you."

"I think I just figured it out on my own."

"I'm using her, for the new book. I'm studying her, the way she talks, the way she thinks."

"The way she makes love?"

"I let it go too far. Boundaries got blurred. I'm sorry."

Anne looks at him, at that face, telling her that his work is more important than their marriage. Or is he just using that as an excuse to get his rocks off? She slaps him hard, so hard her palm burns. She stands there for a moment, not quite believing what's happening. It's all so wrong—that their marriage has come to this. And tomorrow she's going to kill her baby.

"We had everything, Charles, everything. Why . . . why?"

He puts a hand on her shoulder.

"Don't touch me! Don't you dare touch me!"

Charles looks her right in the eye. "I won't touch her again, that's over. I promise you that. But try to understand. The last book was hell, and the truth is I'm afraid to let her go. I've grown dependent on her for this new book, in some way I don't really understand. This is for our future."

Anne can feel his fear and it makes *her* afraid. She's confused and weary and soiled. She believes him—he is using the girl for his new book—but what kind of man does that make him?

"I don't ever want her to set foot in this apartment again."

"Fair enough. And I promise you that as soon as the book is finished, she'll be out of our lives forever."

Anne feels the fight go out of her. The fact that Emma is inspiring him hurts the most. A fuck is one thing, but that Emma could be such a part of his work, in a way that she's never been . . . Suddenly all Anne wants is for him to be out of her sight, to be alone. A bath, a hot bath.

"I don't know, Charles, I honestly don't know."

"I love you, Anne, and I'm very sorry."

Without answering, Anne walks past him, through the bedroom and into the bathroom, locking the door behind her.

.   .   .

Charles races down the hallway toward the elevator. The door is closing—he sticks out his arm to stop it. It rolls open and he steps in. Emma is backed into the corner, her forearm covered with bloody scratches.

"Did Anne do that?"

She quickly rolls down her sleeve. "Leave me alone."

My God, she did it to herself.

"I'm so sorry you had to go through that."

She stares straight ahead as the elevator begins its descent.

"Emma, talk to me."

"There's nothing to say."

"There's everything to say."

"Go fuck yourself."

"Be reasonable."

"Don't you mean obedient?"

And she turns on him, fierce. A bloodstain appears on her sleeve. They both notice it. She turns away, breathing in quick, shallow gulps, her lower lip trembling. She might leave town, and the book isn't finished; he needs her, needs to protect her—she's suicidal, isn't she?

"Emma, listen to me. I'm going to tell Anne I want a divorce."

Emma tries to disguise her shock, and her hope—but it sparks in her eyes. She just keeps staring straight ahead. Charles lets his words sink in.

"And from now on, we'll work at your place. You'll never have to see her again. Emma, you must know you're more important to me than she is. Didn't we prove that today?"

Still she won't look at him.

"I love you, Emma. But I won't force you to do anything. It's all up to you."

The elevator doors open. Emma turns and looks at Charles, a dare in her eyes. Then she walks away.

34

AT THIS HOUR, in the dark belly of night, the streetlights of Central Park glitter like lost jewels. Charles stands at the window in his study, tracing the path of a lone taxicab as it makes its way beneath the spindly web of trees. He hopes that whoever is in the cab is beautiful and young and that the night holds them gently.

Charles turns away from the window and reaches for the bottle of Chivas on his desk. He pours himself another drink and takes a long, slow sip. The only light comes from a small desk lamp with a green glass shade. Charles is comfortable in its shadows.

It isn't really Emma's book anymore. He's changed virtually every sentence, suggested whole scenes, molded Zack, given the mother complexity and pathos. It's written in his style; it has his voice. It's his book now. Besides, he needs it so much more than she does. It's his resurrection. If Emma publishes the book, it will destroy her. Her past will come out, the media will create a sideshow, and she'll be turned into a freak: The Girl Who Murdered Her Mother. She'll have a psychotic break. What had the psychiatrist said? Incipient schizophrenia. Charles has to protect her. She's all alone in the world.

He walks into the outer office. She's left a sweater, a simple gray cardigan, on the back of her chair. He picks it up and feels the wool, running it slowly between his fingers. Then he presses his face into the sweater, and smells Emma, his Emma, and thinks of their day together, their lovemaking. They gave each other so much of themselves—from the beginning, really. What he'll do is set up some kind of fund for her, from the earnings. He'll call his old Dartmouth classmate, Dan Leber, he's one of the best psychiatrists in the city. When they finish their work, Emma will need a good long rest somewhere, somewhere in the country, somewhere peaceful.

Charles goes back to his desk and pours himself another two fingers of Chivas, which he downs in a swallow. He'll have to be very careful from here on in. If he can just keep things on keel for another two weeks, that's all the time he needs, he's that close. Portia wrote him a letter, demanding to see the book. And so he'll show her what he has. He gathers up the manuscript and slides it into a manila envelope. He switches on his computer, its screen bathing him in a ghostly glow, and types the title page:

The Sky Is Falling

A novel

by

Charles Davis

For the briefest time, between the reveler's last hour and the laborer's first, Manhattan feels like a ghost town. In the unearthly calm and quiet, Charles walks out of his building with the manila envelope under his arm. The mailbox is a block away, but it feels like a mile. Charles loves the stillness, the sense of having stepped into a world with its own rules. Of course he's doing the right thing, the right thing for everyone. He reaches the mailbox and opens it. For a moment he hesitates, and then he drops in the envelope and the box clangs shut.

35

ANNE CAN'T SIT STILL. She's overwhelmed by anxiety, and she hates this overdecorated suite at Kayla's hotel. She wants to rip down the hideous window treatments—acres of swag-infested paisley. The coffee on the room-service tray is cold but she takes another gulp anyway, lights a Kent, and flicks on the television. She races through the channels until they blur into a vomitous kaleidoscope of American culture. She walks into one of the enormous bathrooms and turns on a hot bath. Then she turns it off. She tosses her cigarette into the toilet. When she walks back out into the living room Kayla is standing there.

"You look strung out," Kayla says.

"Oh, I'm way beyond strung out."

The two friends hug long and hard.

"It'll all be over in a few hours. Sit down," Kayla says, picking up the phone. "Yes, could you send up a big pot of mint tea, please? . . . I said sit down."

Anne obeys. Only Kayla could look so good fresh off the red-eye; relaxed and fit in faded jeans, a white T-shirt, and a navy cashmere blazer—she calls it her Goldie Hawn uniform. Her frizzy hair erupts around her round face, which—to the untrained eye—looks makeup-free. She finds Mozart on the radio, takes off her blazer, kneels, pulls off Anne's flats and begins to give her an expert foot massage. Anne closes her eyes and rests her head against the back of the sofa.

"Thanks for coming, Kayla."

"You couldn't have kept me away. I'm worried about you."

"I'll be okay."

"You sure?"

Anne nods.

"I called my 'friend,' " Kayla says.

"Will she take the job?"

"She will. It's not going to be cheap, though."

"I don't care what it costs," Anne says.

Anne and Kayla are the only people in the clinic waiting room. It's a pleasant room painted in mellow tones; Bach plays softly. Dr. Arnold comes out. She's reassuring, maternal, with shoulder-length gray hair superbly cut, a handsome face, warm gray eyes. She greets them, gives Anne a Valium, explains the procedure, tells her she'll be ready in about twenty minutes.

Anne is calmer. She and Kayla sit there in silence. What is there to say?

And then Anne's body starts to tremble. Her face contorts and the tears come, thick and salty. Now she's rocking back and forth and shaking and moaning and Kayla is afraid she's having a convulsion of some kind. She tries to put her arms around her but Anne pushes her away and runs out of the office and Kayla races after her and Anne falls in the hallway and Kayla can hear her knee crack against the floor. She clambers up and runs past the receptionist and out onto the street. Kayla follows. It's starting to rain, a gusty rain that sends leaves and bits of trash swirling through the air.

Passersby turn and stare as Anne runs past them. Kayla struggles not to lose sight of her.

And then she does.

Kayla stands on the street corner, frantic, scanning, searching, afraid at any second she's going to hear the screech of tires, a thud, a scream.

There's a church behind her, a beautiful stone church. She sprints up the steps and opens the heavy wooden doors. The vaulted sanctuary is hushed, her footfalls echo, she smells incense and candles. It takes her eyes a moment to adjust to the dim light pouring through stained glass. Half a dozen worshipers are scattered among the front pews, praying silently. No Anne. Then she hears a noise. She walks silently down the center aisle. Anne is lying in the second to last pew, curled in on herself like a cat, her body heaving with choked sobs.

36

IT'S GUSTING RAIN and Charles is huddled at a pay phone, listening to the ring on the other end of the line and keeping his eyes on the windows of Emma's apartment a block away. He can see the faint glow of her bedside lamp, the one shaped like three puppies. He forgot his umbrella and water drips down the back of his neck. He reaches into his pocket and pulls out his mono-grammed silver flask—a long-ago gift from Nina—and takes a deep swallow of Scotch. He knows she's in there, listening to the phone ring, letting it go unanswered. He can *feel* her at the other end of the line, looking at the phone, thinking of him, playing her game. Let her play it, he thinks as he hangs up yet again, let her have her little satisfaction. He'll play the supplicant if that's what it takes.

From outside, her apartment looks dry and cozy. He imagines going there, her handing him a rough towel, watching as he dries his hair. Get out of those soggy clothes, she'd say, and her words would excite them both. He would slowly undress in the warmth of her apartment, while she made a pot of tea. They would get in bed together and hold each other and talk. He might even explain to her about the book, why it is his, how this is best for them both. And then slowly, inevitably, they would make love and everything would be all right.

The wind gusts, and he huddles tight under the meager shelter. He has to keep watching, of course, in case she decides to do something rash. Hurt herself. It's reassuring that her line is never busy, that she isn't making calls. But who would she call? She has no friends. She'll come back.

Charles takes another pull from the flask. Some asshole, a downtown degenerate with a pierced lip, what else, appears and indicates he wants to use the phone. Charles has to think fast. It's too soon to call Emma back. But he can't give up this spot.

"I'll be a little while," Charles says. Guy looks like a cadaver. Probably a junkie. Charles drops in another quarter and dials his answering machine. When he hears Portia's voice, his pulse starts to race.

"Charles, call me immediately."

He hangs up and turns to the sleazy addict, who's lighting a cigarette in the rain. A fancy European cigarette. Probably stole them.

"I have to make another call."

"Whatever."

Some people just can't take a hint. Charles uses his credit card to call Portia. She answers halfway through the first ring.

"Charles?"

"Yes, it's me."

"I need to talk to you. I want you to come up here."

"Did you get my manuscript?"

"Yes."

"Well?"

"I'll expect you here tomorrow for a late lunch."

And then she hangs up.

What a strange response. Suddenly Charles is afraid, afraid that

Portia hates the book. The wind gusts, and he's lashed by rain. He's soaked, standing there holding the dead receiver. The junkie takes a step forward.

"All right, it's yours," Charles says, moving away from the phone. He isn't sure where to go. He hears Portia's voice. Can he leave Emma alone for the day? He moves down the street toward her apartment, staying close to the buildings, pressing against them. What if she looks out the window and sees him? He ducks into a shallow doorway and finishes his whiskey. It's a good vantage point. He'll just stay here, keep watching her window, make sure she doesn't go out, doesn't disappear—that's a good plan.

37

CHARLES WAKES UP ON on the couch in his office, fully clothed. Anne spent the weekend at her friend Kayla's hotel suite—passive aggression disguised as female bonding. Fine—she's out of his hair. Charles calls for his car. He makes it up the Thruway in record time, fighting a headachy hangover all the way. The day is gray and humid, the landscape bare and uninspiring; with the leaves gone, all the dreary malls and self-storage barns leap out at him. He gets off the Thruway and heads deep into the forest. There's no sign of human life for many miles, as if the world has ended and he's the last man left. Just endless woods, woods that could swallow you up without anyone knowing it.

Charles finally reaches Portia's cabin. Smoke is coming from its chimney; a lamp glows inside; hardy mums bloom in haphazard clumps around the yard. He finds Portia slumped in her favorite chair—a cigarette in her mouth, a mug of coffee beside her, half-glasses perched on the end of her nose—reading his manuscript.

"You're early," she says, without looking up.

"I suppose that means lunch isn't ready yet."

"Lunch is somewhere out there in the lake." She puts down the manuscript and picks up her cane. "Let's go."

In California they call it earthquake weather, these gray, still, unseasonably humid days. Good weather for going insane. Carrying the fishing rods, Charles follows Portia down the wooden steps that wind down the cliff to the lake. They walk out onto the old dock—it wobbles and creaks beneath them—and climb into Portia's battered rowboat. A sad little puddle sits in the bottom of the boat and Charles can feel the water seep into his socks. Portia takes the oars and slowly begins to row them out onto the deserted lake. The suffocating silence is broken only by the rhythmic squeak of the oarlocks. From somewhere deep in the forest comes the plaintive cry of a distant bird—or is it a coyote? The moist air and low clouds make it hard to breathe, as if the sky were a damp blanket slowly descending over the earth.

When they reach the middle of the lake, Portia ships the oars and expertly casts her fishing line.

"Ten years ago the lake would have been frozen over by this time. Winter feels like summer and summer feels like hell. The day is coming when the living will envy the dead, mark my words. In the meantime, I wish I could stop caring so much."

She reels in her line and casts off again.

"I've reread it three times. I didn't know I could still be so moved by the written word. That boy, that poor lost child . . . and his mother—what a harrowing creation. Haunting, simply haunting. I haven't felt this way since I first read *your* work."

"What do you mean?"

"I mean you didn't write it."

Charles laughs uneasily. "Of course I wrote it. Who else could have written it?"

"Don't play games with me, Charles. Did you really think you could deceive me?"

"I didn't come all the way up here to listen to this."

"What did you come up here for? To be reassured that you could pass off this work as your own? To the one person who knows your writing best? To be told that you're a genius, that you're finally, gloriously, out of the slump you've been in for the past ten years?"

"Stop it."

"That you've found your voice again, that you're writing something with heart and soul and real life again, something that matters, something—"

"*I said stop it!*"

"I'll stop when you start telling me the truth."

There's a long silence, and then that distant cry echoes across the lake. Charles can't bring himself to look at Portia and so he looks down at his hands. They look veined and blotchy and old.

"I fell in love with her. She made me feel alive again. . . . I wanted to help her."

"Help her?"

Charles thinks of Emma sitting at his library table, writing, her face lit from within. He sees a stray lock of hair tumble across her face, remembers that mischievous glint in her eye when she tasted one of his french fries, feels a momentary ache for her body. He does love her. And he's gone terribly wrong.

"I gave Nina the manuscript, took Emma's name off it so it would get a fair reading. She thought it was mine. She said it was the great book everyone's been waiting for me to write."

"But it isn't."

Charles finally looks up at Portia.

"And you can't pretend it is," she says.

He looks out over the lake and wonders what has brought him to this place.

"No, I can't," he says simply. He reaches over the side and trails his hand in the cold, numbing water. Then he looks at Portia. There's a challenge in her eyes, but also something else. Is it forgiveness? Or at least understanding? Her expression softens. She does understand. And she still loves him. He can redeem himself. Charles knows what he has to do: he has to go back to New York and make things right.

Suddenly there's a sharp pull on Portia's line. She stands up to reel in the fish and loses her balance. The boat starts to rock and she struggles to regain her footing, shoots Charles a beseeching look. He stands up to help—and the boat rocks more violently. Portia panics, drops the fishing rod, bangs her knee against the gunwale, and begins to tumble forward, toward the frigid water. For one split second Charles is elated: No one can survive in that water; she'll go into shock, die quickly, cleanly. He'll be home free; the book will be his.

And then he lunges forward, grabs her, and pulls her to safety.

Charles holds her fast. They're both breathing heavily, afraid to move, waiting for the boat to stop pitching. Slowly it steadies itself. Charles takes a deep breath and gingerly moves back to his seat.

Portia tries to disguise how shook up she is. She pulls out a Pall Mall and sticks it between her lips. She lights a match and just before she holds the flame to the cigarette, she looks over at Charles. "I've never once been wrong about you."

Charles helps Portia out of the rowboat and secures it to the dock. She follows him across the patch of rocky shoreline. As they climb the steps, the only sound is their footfalls on the old wood. Charles feels emptied out, emotionless; speech seems an impossible effort—and what is there to say? Behind him he hears Portia's labored breathing as she climbs, and her labored steps, her old feet carrying her old body. They near the halfway point, where the stairs turn and there's a small landing.

"I've got one of my chicken pot pies in the freezer, I'll stick it in the oven," she says.

Charles reaches the landing and starts up the final stretch. Portia stops a moment, leaning against the rail, sucking air.

"God bless R. J. Reynolds," she says.

Charles turns and looks at her.

"You really should think about quitting," he says.

And then he pushes her.

38

ANNE IS THINKING seriously about single motherhood as her cab struggles through traffic. The weekend with Kayla was rejuvenating: room-service meals, silly television shows, long talks—and a chance to gain some perspective on the situation with Charles. Divorce would be a big fat mess, of course, and Anne hates the thought of giving up, just hates it. But she'll be damned if she'll let Charles take her and her child down with him. He wasn't at the apartment this morning when she went home to change for work, and it was obvious he'd been living in his office; the room was littered with tangled blankets, take-out food containers, and empty bottles of Scotch. The cab runs a light and a horn blares and she instinctively grabs the door handle—someone has stuck a wad of fresh chewing gum under it.

For about six months she's been thinking of moving her company downtown, creating a twenty-first-century workplace that would generate a lot of press and a lot of prestige for Anne Turner Inc. A real estate agent called to let her know about two adjoining warehouses with a large hidden courtyard between them. Anne was intrigued. An architect she's interested in, a young Italian woman who's creating a stir with her ravishing lofts and Silicon Alley offices, is going to look at the properties with her. Anne has to be at the Hilton in an hour, really should have scheduled this at another time, but she wants her days to be jammed beyond reason.

Anne hops out of the cab in frustration and walks the last six blocks. The buildings are in the far West Twenties, near the Hudson River. The architect and the real estate agent are standing out front. The agent is an older man, tweedy and reserved. Gabriella, the architect, is pulled together in that uniquely Milanese way— belted black cashmere coat, black hair in a striking geometric cut—all postmodern cool.

The agent leads them through the two vacant buildings, with vast open floors and fantastic old mullioned windows that look out at the river and New Jersey beyond. The courtyard is a junk heap but has the kind of potential that thrills Anne. She imagines it as a garden, an unexpected oasis for her staff, with shade trees and rushing water.

The tour over, the three of them stand in front of the building.

"Why don't you let your imagination go crazy, and call me next week," Anne says to Gabriella.

Gabriella nods and lights a cigarette. She looks up at the buildings. "Fantastic."

"I'm sorry I have to run," Anne says.

"I am embarrassed," Gabriella says with a charming smile. She pulls out an Italian edition of *Life and Liberty*. "Your husband's work, it means so much to me. I found this first edition. If he would sign it, please?"

The day is humid and still, the world covered with low clouds; at the end of the street the river is wide and gray. Anne hears children's voices from the corner playground. She looks down at Charles's book, runs her hand over the jacket. How old was she when she first read *Life and Liberty* and was so transported by it? For a moment she thinks she might cry.

"I know he'll be happy to sign this. I'll messenger it down to you by the end of the week," Anne says. Then she steps off the curb and hails a taxi.

Anne pushes through the Hilton's revolving doors and strides up the moving escalator to the ballroom. She's late for the luncheon—considered skipping it, but it's important—for the Children's Defense Fund. She wrote them a check, but wants to be here in person, to feel like a part of the work they do, to connect. And to be seen. It's very important for her to be seen these days, for people to know she's out there doing her job, that everything is fine.

As she crosses the mezzanine she runs into Nina Bradley.

The two women stand looking at each other across all the years, all the dinners, all the laughs. Anne always thought of Nina as an extension of Charles in some funny way—the two of them were so close, almost like siblings.

"I'm so sorry," Anne says.

"You have nothing to apologize for."

"Thank you. You're very generous."

Nina smiles—beautiful Nina. "I need some time, Anne." Then she starts into the ballroom.

Anne doesn't want to lose her. There are few people whose opinion she trusts more.

"Nina?" she calls. Nina turns and Anne lowers her voice: "His new book, is it really that good?"

Nina looks at Anne for a long moment. "Yes," she says.

And then she walks away.

Anne stands there in the cold expanse and a chill runs up her neck. She heads into the ballroom, hoping she'll be able to sit still through the lunch.

39

EMMA IS CURLED UP in bed with all the lights off, staring at a paint chip on the wall. She hasn't eaten in two days, hasn't bathed in a while. The red neon glow streams in the window and she can hear voices down on the street below, happy voices, and all Emma wants to do is die. She feels like she's back in the hospital, during those endless early months when she lay on her bed unable to move and the doctors came and talked to her and she couldn't answer because she didn't understand what they were saying, because the words made no sense, coming from so far away, from that other world. Emma's world ends, then and now, at the edge of her bed, just falls away, black and hopeless.

After a weekend of the phone constantly ringing, Charles hasn't called once all day. He's given up, come to his senses. Why would he ever leave a woman like Anne Turner for a girl like her, a girl with no family, no breeding, no education, a BadGirlSickGirl. Emma shrinks further into herself on the bed. She turns and gets caught up in the tangle of bedclothes; they're sweaty and dirty and dank and all she wants is the energy to climb up to the roof and jump, fly into nothingness—sweet release.

And then there's a knock on the door.

"Emma? It's me."

Emma stumbles out of bed and switches on a light. The place is a mess. She frantically straightens the bed, shoves papers under the sofa.

"Emma?"

"Coming," she calls, slipping on a robe over her T-shirt and panties. She takes a deep breath and opens the door.

How strange he looks—sunken and tortured and scared. Does she smell whiskey on his breath? He needs her as much as she needs him—that's it! These days apart have been an equal agony for her poor Charles.

He kicks the door closed behind him and pushes her against the wall and kisses her hard, his body pressing insistently into hers. He opens her robe and grabs her panties in his fist and rips them and pushes down his pants and enters her. His thrusts are violent and Emma is scared by his need and she's knocking into the wall and she wants him to stop and take her to the bed and make gentle love to her but still he thrusts and thrusts—and then there's nothing but his smell and his tongue and his cock and she wraps her legs and arms around him and thrusts back again and again and again, matching his violence with her own.

It's after one in the morning when Charles finally walks in the front door. The apartment is dark. He's so exhausted; he's never been this exhausted before—beyond thought, beyond feeling. He only wants to sleep, to sleep and wake up in a better world. He walks into the living room and over to the bar. He pours himself a stiff Scotch and downs it. That moment—his hands pushing Portia—floods back and he shudders. He can smell himself, rank with sweat and fear. What has he done?

"Welcome home."

Charles spins around to see Anne sitting on the couch by the fireplace. In the dim light, her face looks hard and angular. He has a sudden urge to confess, to be forgiven, absolved, cleansed. No. That would destroy everything.

"I didn't see you there," he says.

"I didn't expect you would. Hard night?"

"Let's not be childish, Anne."

"No, let's not. Let's be very adult. How much longer do you need to finish your book?"

"About two weeks."

"Today's Monday. On Friday I'll leave for a week in Los Angeles. Kayla and I have some business plans. When I come back, I want her out of your life."

"I appreciate this."

"I don't want your appreciation. I want our marriage back."

The world goes on and people like Anne put one foot in front of the other and do what they have to do.

"So do I, darling," he says.

"I'm three months pregnant."

Charles sits beside Anne and she recoils slightly—his smell, no doubt. He takes her hand and holds it to his cheek, smells it, kisses it. Then he gently touches her stomach.

"Thank you . . . for everything," he says.

They sit there without speaking. It's been such a long day. But worth it. He'll deliver a great book—for Anne, for their child, for the man he once was and still at heart remains.

40

I T ' S   E A R L Y ,   B U T Emma is already at her typewriter. She's
exhausted, hasn't even dressed yet, but Charles will be arriving
soon and she wants him to find her at work. They're nearing the
end of the book and she's finding it almost impossible to write. She
wants the boy, Zack, to get away from his mother, escape their
squalid, sorry life. She imagines him rescued by his aunt, a shad-
owy but important character in the book. Rescued, taken away—as
she hadn't been. She can see him playing in the sun on the fresh
green lawn of his aunt's house. Safe. Happy. Saved.

But no, Charles won't hear of it. He says it would read like a
tacked-on Hollywood ending; it would lack dramatic punch and
tragic resonance, sabotage the climax they'd been building up to.
He's been fierce and unrelenting on this point, has mocked all of
her objections. There's only one way to end it, he insists: have
Zack kill his mother. Not pretty, but honest. Bold. Horrifying.

·   ·   ·

That March night, as the soft snow fell outside the window, the small town lay curled in on itself and Emma lay coiled on her bed, her body covered with wounds and welts, trembling with fear and rage, staring at her bedroom door, barricaded with all the room's furniture, waiting, almost afraid to breathe, her mother, *the devil*, in the middle of a three-day speed-fueled fit, a fury, and then suddenly—she must have crept close—a crashing as she threw her skinny venomous body against the door again and again and again, screaming, and the furniture started to slide across the floor and her mother started to laugh and Emma realized with a sudden clarity that her mother was insane and so was she, they were both crazy, *sick crazy,* and she hated her mother for making her crazy, wanted only to kill her, and then the door was halfway open and Emma looked out at the snow and it was so pretty. . . .

And so Emma writes, each word like blood, and dreams of when it will be over. And then what? She hears his key in the door and quickly lowers her head, hoping to feel his lips on her neck. Instead he says, "Good morning," and moves to the kitchen area.

"Good morning," Emma says, looking up. Charles hasn't shaved, his hair is greasy, and there are dark circles under his eyes. He looks drawn and bloated at the same time. He's carrying a shopping bag, which he sets down on the counter. Some food, some wonderful treats, Emma thinks. But he reaches into the bag and lifts out a fishbowl.

"What's that?" Emma asks.

Charles pulls out a water-filled plastic bag in which two goldfish are swimming and dumps them into the bowl. "Goldfish." He holds up the bowl like a proud little kid. "Are you all right, Emma?"

"Why goldfish?"

"Impulse. I had them when I was a boy." Charles sets the bowl on the counter and studies the fish. "Beautiful, aren't they?"

Emma nods.

"It's amazing they don't go mad, swimming around and around in such a small space all their lives," he says.

"How would we know if they did?"

"Go mad?"

"Yes."

He lights a cigarette.

"Did you ever have fish?" he asks.

Emma shakes her head.

"Are you sure?"

"Positive."

"For some reason, I imagined you as the kind of girl who would have kept fish. A turtle maybe?"

"No."

"I thought it might be interesting if Zack had them."

"In the book?"

"Yes, silly. In the book. Don't you think a child in his position would try to create a world, even a world as small as a fishbowl, where he could be in control? Where there was no chaos and pain, just gentle swimming hour after hour?"

Emma doesn't answer.

"Am I working you too hard, Emma?"

"No."

"I know this is all terribly complicated, with Anne and the book and us. I'm sorry to put you through it."

He comes toward her and she prays he'll touch her, stroke her. But when he gets close he turns and walks into the bathroom.

"I look a wreck, don't I?" he asks.

"A little tired," Emma says.

"It is a strain." He goes and lies on her bed. "Only one thing to do, get to work. Cures all ills. Read me what you've got."

Emma looks at the goldfish, swimming in restless circles around the small glass bowl. Why are they looking at her like that?

41

ANNE WATCHES CHARLES as he sits at the kitchen table and reads Portia's obituary. He looks so shocked, so solemn.

According to the *New York Times* Portia fell from an outdoor staircase and down a rock ledge. Her decomposing body was discovered by two hikers. Animals had been at it. Anne is fascinated by these morbid details—the ignominious ending of an illustrious life. And then there's something about accidental death—the reminder of how short the distance is from here to there, how it can be crossed in an instant, the ultimate one-way street. The way the kitchen looks in the morning light, the taste of her coffee, seem altered somehow.

Anne reminds herself that Charles has lost the person he trusted most. "I'm sorry," she says.

"She would have wanted to die like that, quickly, by her lake."

"She had a long and wonderful life," Anne says, feeling slightly idiotic, as she always does when she has to summon up dishonest emotion.

"At least now I can dedicate the new book to her. After *Life and Liberty*, she never let me do that again."

Charles carries Anne's bags down to the car. The day is tangy and bright. Charles is blinking against the sunlight, shading his eyes. Hung over. Probably thinking about Emma, his so-called inspiration. He made his bed; now he and his creepy little muse can sleep in it.

"I hope your work goes well," Anne says.

"And yours," Charles answers, distracted, looking around, almost as if he's paranoid.

They cross the sidewalk, the driver takes Anne's bags, and she and Charles look at each other.

"I am sorry about Portia," Anne says.

"So am I."

Anne reaches up and touches Charles's cheek lightly and then turns and gets in the car.

Los Angeles is just a little too close to home for Anne—she can't face her mother, not this week—but Kayla's Spanish-style spread in Santa Monica is warm and comfortable. She takes a long swim and a short nap, and when Kayla comes home Anne makes them a salad and an omelette.

At nine on the dot the young woman arrives. She's not what Anne expected—she wears glasses, a black turtleneck, loose jeans, and espadrilles; her hair is tucked up in a barrette. But there's no disguising her beauty and cool cunning. The three of them sit around the oak table in the kitchen for two hours and twenty minutes, deep in discussion.

"I think I'm going to enjoy Cambridge," the woman says finally, gathering up her notes.

Anne opens her purse and takes out an envelope filled with twenty thousand dollars in crisp hundreds. She hands it to the young woman, who shakes her hand and leaves.

42

WHEN EMMA LOOKS UP from her desk, Charles is standing there, a leather suitcase in one hand. He has on a brown hunting jacket and dark gloves. He tosses the suitcase onto her bed.

"I'm staying down here this week," he says.

He's staying at her apartment. She'll fall asleep with him beside her, and when she wakes up in the middle of the night he'll be there. There'll be lots of work, of course, but also times when they'll lie around reading or cook pasta or laugh at something silly.

"We have to stay focused on the work, Emma. This is the crucial week. We'll be at it twenty-four hours a day if we have to."

There'll be no laughs. He'll be bearing down on her relentlessly. The apartment will become a cage.

The motherfucker.

"You understand, don't you, Emma?"

Emma looks down at her writing. He'll only be here for a week and then she'll have the one thing she wants as much as she wants Charles—her book. She does still want it, doesn't she?

"I understand," she says.

Charles opens his suitcase and Emma sees that his clothes are jammed in, unpressed, a jumble. He empties out one of her dresser drawers. "Portia Damron died," he says as he begins to shove his clothes into the drawer.

Portia. That remarkable old woman who came to his office that day, his mentor and idol. Emma remembers her face, ancient and deeply lined, her eyes dancing with wisdom and mischief. She showed such interest in Emma, warned her not to let Charles take advantage of her. Dead.

"How did she die?"

Charles finishes unpacking his clothes and takes a small leather kit into the bathroom. "She fell," he says.

"Fell?"

"At her place up in the Adirondacks. I warned her that old stairway down to the lake was crumbling. She never listened."

"At least it was quick," Emma says.

Charles returns from the bathroom and stands over her. "We can't be sure of that. She may have broken her legs or her back and been unable to move. There would have been no one to hear her cries for help. She could have lain there for days."

Emma imagines the old woman lying there, helpless, beside the lake, slowly dying. What went through her mind? Was there peace, finally? Or only growing terror?

"Animals had been at her body."

Would the animals have waited until she was dead?

Charles seems so unaffected by his loss. A fire engine shrieks in the distance. Someone's house is on fire. Emma wishes it were cloudy out. The sunshine is so depressing. Her fingernails are dirty. She clasps her hands together beneath the desk.

"Are you sure you want to work today?" she asks.

Charles goes to the kitchen sink and washes his hands. He dries them on the last of the paper towels. She'll have to get more. Finally he turns and leans against the counter. He looks blank somehow, oddly blank.

"Portia would have wanted me to work," he says finally.

The first draft of the ending is nearly finished. Zack stays late at school, hangs out alone in the art room—the teacher lets him; she knows about his situation at home. He's making a collage. And then his mother shows up, drunk, on a tear, and starts in on him, brutally, smacks him to the floor, kicks him in the head, she's killing him—and the scissors gleam in the late afternoon sun. *And the snow was so pretty out the window.*

Charles is stretched out on her bed, reading what she wrote. Emma sits at her desk, waiting for his response. She's so tired that she almost doesn't care. She wants it to be nighttime, when they'll be sharing the bed, climbing in together, and he'll be warm beside her.

"It's not up to your usual standard," he says, putting down the pages.

"I'll rewrite it," she says quickly.

"You know what, it's easier for me to fix it myself."

"But, Charles—"

He sits up and leans forward on his elbows. "Listen to me, Emma. The ending needs some serious help. It's erratic. There are flashes of brilliance and then whole passages that read like they were written by a profoundly disturbed teenager."

The motherfucker.

"Hand me a pencil, would you?"

Emma brings him the pencil. He takes it without looking up at her and immediately begins to write over her words.

"Have you fed the fish?" he asks.

. . .

Emma takes a shower, a quick one. The water stings and she hates the way her skin feels when it's wet, but she wants to be clean for him; she wants to smell nice. She dries herself too quickly; when she puts on her nightgown she feels damp on her thighs and inner arms. She runs a brush through her hair and takes a quick look in the mirror. She tries to smile, but it comes out all strained and weird. She has to stop looking in mirrors.

She steps out of the bathroom and sees that Charles is making up the sofa into a bed.

"It's better this way. No distractions," he says.

Emma nods.

Now he's walking toward her with something in his hand.

"Here," he says.

She looks down and sees two white pills in his palm.

"What are those?"

"Just a mild sedative. I know you haven't been sleeping."

"I don't like to take pills."

"Did you used to? Take pills?"

Emma shakes her head.

"You need rest. You'll feel better. A good, deep sleep." His voice is so soothing. The pills do look comforting, sweet little white pills, they're her friends, yes, yes they are.

Emma takes the pills and Charles hands her a glass of water. He watches as she swallows them.

"Good girl," he says.

The pills don't work. Emma lies awake in the middle of the night, frightened. The Chinese restaurant has turned off its sign. It's so quiet outside, as if the whole city has died. She looks up at the shadows on the ceiling. They're wavy and remind her of water and water reminds her of the goldfish so she closes her eyes. She can hear Charles's rhythmic breathing. She gets up, as quietly as she can, lifting the covers slowly, holding her breath. The floor is so cold and the corners of the room so dark. Gently lowering one foot in front of the other, she crosses to the sofa. She looks down at him, curled up on his side like a little boy. He has the blanket pulled up to his chin and the tiniest smile flickers at the corners of his mouth. What would happen if she held a pillow over his face and pressed as hard as she could? She wants to crawl in beside him, but she doesn't. She just stands there in the dark looking at him, waiting for morning to come.

Where are her notes? She wrote a page of notes to herself last night, last thing, right before her shower, and left it next to the typewriter. Now she can't find it. She looks through all the papers on the desk.

"Charles, have you seen my notes?"

He's sitting on the sofa, working on the manuscript, and he doesn't look up. "No," he says. Like it's no big deal.

Emma is sure she saw the page on the desk earlier this morning. Where is it?

"I just saw it here."

He still doesn't look up. "Then it must still be there."

"But it isn't."

Finally he looks up.

"Well, maybe it folded itself into a paper airplane and flew out the window. Emma, what is wrong with you this morning?"

"Those pills didn't work."

He puts down the manuscript and looks at her.

"I'm sorry," he says, looking concerned. "You should have told me earlier. You must be exhausted. Don't worry about the notes; they'll turn up."

Of course they will. It's only a page of notes. Anyway, Charles will fix the chapter. He's been so helpful with the book. Emma feels silly. For getting so upset. And she's so tired, almost too tired to care.

"Why don't you knock off and take a nap?"

Emma does. She crawls back into bed with her clothes on and shuts her eyes. The bed is so soft and the sounds of the city so lulling. Charles is here and she can sleep.

43

PORTIA'S MEMORIAL SERVICE is at the Dartmouth Club. Charles has been asked to speak, of course. He leaves Emma early in the morning and takes a cab back to the apartment. He takes the book with him. It's a cloudy morning with a chill in the air. As the cab crawls through traffic, he tries to compose a speech of some kind, but images of that day—*walking down the rickety steps, the low gray sky*—crowd his mind.

It's strange to arrive at his own building as a visitor. The apartment feels eerily calm, as if everyone had left in a hurry, and his office is a mess, correspondence piling up, tangled bedding spilling off the couch. He carefully locks the manuscript in his desk.

In the kitchen he makes himself a cup of strong black coffee and then spikes it with Scotch. It was Portia who introduced him to the pleasures of an early morning spike—*climbing into the battered rowboat, the cold water seeping into his socks, the cry of a distant bird.*

The master bedroom looks perfect, like a page out of an

Anne Turner catalog—except that the tulips on Anne's night table are limp and have dropped most of their petals. In the bathroom, he looks for something to lessen the sense of dread—he can't take the Xanax he's giving Emma; it makes him too groggy. He opens the medicine chest. The sparkling shelves look like a magazine ad: shiny tweezers, opaque glass jars, Q-Tips, and cotton balls. It's all so fucking artful and antiseptic. He sweeps his hand over a shelf, knocking everything down onto the counter in a spray of broken glass and spilled mouthwash and witch hazel.

After putting on a dark wool suit, Charles decides to walk down to the Dartmouth Club. The exercise will clear his head and calm him down. He goes only a few blocks before he starts to sweat. The sun has come out and burned away the morning chill, the day is turning out to be unseasonably warm and humid. Can it really be late November? "Winter feels like summer and summer feels like hell," Portia had said. "The day is coming when the living will envy the dead." He wishes he'd worn a lighter suit; the scarf around his neck is itchy; he's dazed. The sun is blinding, glinting off metallic surfaces, and he didn't bring sunglasses. Somewhere below Columbus Circle he ducks into a discount pharmacy. The place is huge and assaultive. He grabs the first pair of sunglasses off the rack, tosses the cashier a twenty-dollar bill and walks out.

The sunglasses help—soften the sharp edges, a barrier from the world. It's getting late and he still has no idea what he'll say. He needs to sit and organize his thoughts. There's a small plaza in front of an office tower; he sits on a hard bench. There are so many people everywhere, they're all around him, moving; he's fidgety, can't concentrate—*the squeak of the oarlocks, the flat gray of the water, the pine trees rising from the shore.*

There's no shade in the bleak little plaza and his heart is pounding in his chest and his mouth is parched. There's a man dressed like a clown handing out flyers, he has Bozo hair and a red plastic nose. He turns and gives Charles a grotesque smile. Charles looks away. Sitting on a bench across from him is a young woman reading a book. Charles squints to make out the title: *Jane Eyre*. The girl is oblivious to the world, her lips parted; she looks a little like Emma, with a wide brow, large eyes, and that intense concentration. She reaches up and brushes a lock of hair from her face— *climbing out of the boat, their slow silent walk across the shore, his foot on the weathered gray step, a cold breeze on the back of his neck . . .*

Charles shudders and stands up. People stream by him as if he isn't there. He walks to a pay phone on the corner and dials Emma's number. There's a lot of traffic and he has a hard time hearing the ringing over the rumble and honking. When Emma finally picks up, she sounds half asleep.

"It's me," he says.

"Where are you?"

"What are we doing, Emma?"

Charles looks out at the people rushing by. They're so filled with purpose, as if it all mattered. Why are they all moving so quickly?

"Should you go away, Emma?"

"Go away?"

"Just leave New York. Today."

A cab with its radio blaring stops at the light.

"I'm sorry, Charles, I can't hear you."

"Leave today."

"I can't hear you."

The light changes and the cab speeds off.

"I don't feel well, Emma."

Charles thinks he might throw up. He needs water.

"You miss Portia."

"Yes."

Charles presses his cheek against the cool metal of the booth.

"I love you, Emma."

There's a long pause.

"Do you really?"

"Yes."

"I'm so tired, Charles."

"I have to get to the service."

"Are you coming down here after?"

A well-dressed middle-aged woman stands nearby, waiting for the phone. Does she recognize him? Of course she does. Charles straightens up.

"Charles, are you there?"

"I'll come down after the service."

It's getting late. He races east and then down Vanderbilt Avenue to the club. He goes into the men's room and is shocked at how cheap and ridiculous the sunglasses look. He takes them off. His eyes are bloodshot. He takes a long drink of water, cupping his palm under the faucet.

The memorial service has already begun. He slips into the hall, a wood-paneled room with a vaulted ceiling. An old man is reading a Rilke poem. A murmur goes around the room as Charles makes his way up to a front pew. Who are all these people? What can they tell? He forces himself to take deep breaths. Why the hell do they have the heat on in this weather? He's suffocating. His suit chafes and he has to piss. Why didn't he piss when he was in the men's room? And then he hears the old man say his name and he realizes everyone is waiting for him to go up and say something about Portia.

He gets up to walk to the front of the room—*the splintering sound as the wood gives way and her body tumbles over backward, her mouth struggling to form words, her head banging on the rock, her body falling, falling. Listening, afraid to breathe. Should he go down there, down to the lake, make sure she's dead?*

He can't raise his eyes from the lectern, doesn't want to see the faces staring up at him. He has to say *something*. How long has he been standing here in silence? It doesn't look right. They're all waiting and the room is so still. Someone coughs and he looks up—a woman in the back row, a handkerchief to her mouth, vaguely familiar, her face filled not with suspicion but with sympathy, sympathy for his loss. He was closer to Portia than any of them. That's what they're all thinking. And they're right.

"When I think of Portia," he begins, "one memory above all others comes back to me. It was my first year at Dartmouth. I hated the place. All those rich kids. Of course I knew who Portia Damron was, but she didn't teach freshmen. It was a Saturday night in the depths of January, and I was feeling pretty sorry for myself. I decided to drive over to the next town where there was a roadside bar that looked welcoming. The place was dark and nobody in there looked like they had a trust fund. I sat down and ordered a Scotch. Down at the far end of the bar I noticed Portia."

Starting down the steps, the low gray sky . . . Hurry, faster, you never know when a hiker will show up, someone could be in the woods on the other side of the lake right now, someone could have seen the whole thing.

"She was deep in conversation with an old fella who looked as if he hadn't drawn a sober breath in forty years. Oh, did I mention she was smoking?" There's a ripple of warm laughter. Charles realizes his eyes are filled with tears; he isn't crying, though; he isn't going to cry. "Suddenly they both slapped bills down on the bar, climbed off their stools, and walked over to a pinball machine. She dropped in a quarter and began to play."

At the bottom—the gray pebbles, and her body, crumpled and twisted, all broken and tiny, like a little broken doll. Stop looking, get away, think think think—make sure she's dead, check the body, make sure she's dead.

"Well, she worked that pinball machine like she was born behind it, twisting and turning and pumping, racking up points. Pretty soon a crowd started to gather, cheering her on. Before you knew it, every last soul in the bar, myself included, was down there. Portia was fierce, pure concentration. Then lights were going off and bells were ringing—she'd broken the all-time record score. We were all screaming and laughing, the place went wild. And Portia? She just kept on playing. But a great big smile broke across her face. That's how I'll always remember her—on that January night, playing pinball, passionate, engaged, *alive.*"

The low gray sky, the lake gently lapping—go look, go look at her body. Her eyes are open. But she's dead, isn't she? One step closer—then he hears it, that wet harsh rattling somewhere in her throat, in her body. Then her eyes move. They look at him. And then he turns, runs up the steps, runs from those eyes—that look—falls twice on the slippery splintered wood. Into the car and he's gone. Gone. It's over. But why does he still hear that sound? Why does he still see her eyes, looking at him?

And now Charles is surrounded by people, people telling him how touched they were by his words and offering condolences and sharing their memories of Portia and boasting how they've followed his career all these years and asking about his next book. He tells them all it's going to be dedicated to Portia. At one point his classmate Dan Leber, the prominent psychiatrist, pulls him aside.

"That was very moving, Charles."

"Thank you."

"She was an amazing teacher. I still have my annotated copy of *Crime and Punishment*. Reread it every five years. Listen, Charles, how's the situation with that young woman you called me about, your secretary?"

From the way he says the words, Charles realizes Leber knows they're having an affair. That's all right; men have affairs all the time.

"It's not improving."

"Well, if you want me to see her, just call."

"I will, Dan. Thank you."

Charles has several glasses of wine and at some point begins to relax. He did it, he got through, no one knows, no one will ever know. All around him, people are trading stories and jokes about Portia and their younger selves, their days in the hills of New Hampshire. Many of them have gone on to successful careers, but none as successful as his. Finally people begin to leave, back to their jobs and their lives. Charles lingers, is one of the last to go. Someone comes up to him, a woman he barely recognizes. A secretary in the English Department?

"You meant more to her than anyone," she says. "She talked

about you all the time. Keep writing for her. Keep her spirit alive.''

He steps out into the afternoon sun. It doesn't feel as oppressive anymore. He thinks of Portia one last time and knows that he can't let her death be in vain. Then he steps off the curb and hails a cab downtown.

44

EMMA WAKES WITH a start. A plane is flying low and the windows are rattling. The sound is getting louder, closer, and she panics—the plane's going to crash into her building, rip the roof off, incinerate her. She calls out for Charles but he doesn't answer. Is he gone? What time is it? She buries her head under the pillow and prays for the sound to stop. It starts to ebb after the plane passes over. She's never been on an airplane.

She has her clothes on. She hates to sleep in her clothes; you feel so weird when you wake up, like you did something wrong, like you were a crazy person sleeping on a park bench. She looks around for Charles, but he isn't there. He's gone. What if he never comes back? Did he call earlier? From a pay phone? How long was she asleep? Out the window it looks like late afternoon. Has she slept the whole day away? She shouldn't have taken another pill—they make her head so thick—but she likes the way they numb her, make things that frighten her fall away. Like flesh falling off a bone.

She pushes off the bed and unsteadily makes her way over to

the kitchen. There's some stale coffee sitting in a saucepan and she turns on the heat. She holds her hands up to the stove and warms them. The heat feels so good. She wonders what it would be like to live in the tropics, to always be warm, to lie in the sun and not think and be warm. She holds her wrist to the flame and a beautiful blister appears.

When she hears his key in the lock, she turns off the gas, licks her wrist, runs her hands through her hair. He can't know she slept like that, lazy girl, sleeping all day, stupid lazy girl, her hair a mess, her clothes rumpled.

He has on a dark suit and he's carrying a white shopping bag. She wonders what's in the shopping bag, but is afraid to ask. His hair is slicked back and he smells of fresh air. He stares at her for a minute and then takes off his coat. "You look terrible," he says.

Yes, she does look terrible. She knows it, but what can she do about it? Her face, her sharp, pointy face. *You could cut cheese with that razor face, dirty monkey girl, face just like your ugly father.* She turns her back to Charles and lets her hair fall in front of her eyes.

"I'm getting some coffee," she says.

"I suppose you've been asleep all afternoon?"

It's that tone of voice again. She hates it, has always hated it. Maybe she should just kill him.

"I took a nap, a few minutes . . ."

"Go sit down. I'll bring you the coffee."

Her desk has been cleaned off. There's nothing there but a stack of clean paper. No notes, no scraps. No book. Her book. None of the pages she's been working on. She *has* been working on them, hasn't she? Why can't she clear her head?

"The pages," she says. "From yesterday. Where are they, Charles?"

He hands her a mug of steaming coffee. "Drink this. It'll make you feel better."

"They were here when I went to sleep. Now they're gone."

"Maybe you shouldn't sleep so much, Emma. Maybe that's the problem."

"I want to see them, read them over."

"The pages are in a safe place."

The pages are in a safe place. But not here. This isn't a safe place. What place is safe? What place is ever safe? "Where are they?" she asks.

Charles grips her shoulders. His hands are strong; she'd forgotten how strong they are. He isn't going to hit her, is he? No, he's just calming her, calming her down. He's being gentle. He cradles her face in his hands. Then he kisses her forehead. "Don't you trust me, little girl?"

Why did he have to ask her that question? His eyes look so caring and she remembers all the wonderful things he's done for her and how his kisses feel and how much she loves him, she loves him so much. She leans her head on his chest and he encircles her with his arms and she feels protected, she wishes they would never move, would just stay this way forever and ever. He strokes her hair over and over again.

He has dinner in the shopping bag. That's all, just dinner. He's humming as he cooks. There's music on, a piano concerto, and the table looks so pretty with candles and napkins. It looks like a home. Zack's mother never set the table. From her desk, Emma can smell garlic and bread, the clean, yeasty smell of fresh bread. It all looks and smells so warm, so safe. *The pages are in a safe place.* But she's at the end of the book now, and it isn't safe there, there in that art classroom in the late afternoon light, Zack and his mother, hateful, horrible mother, hateful horrible dirty mother. But he's going to kill her. He doesn't want to, but he has to, he has no choice, she'll kill him if he doesn't do it first. Any reader will be able to see that. Justifiable homicide. Just kill her, stop her, shut her up, that constant screeching screeching voice. *You funny monkey, worthless piece-of-shit monkey.*

"Soup's on."

She looks up. Charles is sitting at the table, pouring wine.

Smiling. He's smiling. She's in a safe place. It's Mozart, that concerto. The most perfect music ever written, wasn't that what he told her?

"I don't think I should stop," she says. "I'm so close to the end."

"You need food." He pours wine into the glasses, red, rich. "You have to keep your strength up."

She stands up. Her body still feels heavy, heavy and thick, but her head feels light—it's as if she is living in two different worlds at once. There's a vase of flowers on the table. Lilacs, feathery violet lilacs, billowing out of her blue thrift-shop vase. Lilacs in late November. One day, maybe, she'll buy lilacs in late November and raspberries in January. . . . *And the seasons they go 'round and 'round*—that song *she* used to play, used to sing.

She sits and looks at the plate of pasta. It smells like garlic and some herb—what is its name? Charles raises his glass. "To the end," he toasts.

She looks at him sadly. "The end?"

"Your book, you nut. Just kill her off and you're finished, done, free. Chop, chop, a few stabs with the scissors, a little blood, a scream or two and you're free. Nothing some soap and water won't erase. Then you can go home."

"Home?"

"Just make sure little Zack doesn't get too much blood on his face. I've been meaning to tell you that. Readers don't want to see the kid with Mommy's blood all over him."

He sips his wine, looking at her over the rim of the glass with a little smirk on his face. This is his idea of a joke. The motherfucker. *There's so much blood, so much blood everywhere, and it isn't chop-chop, she keeps hitting keeps hitting keeps hitting. And then stuff comes out, comes out of her mother's head.* Emma feels her stomach spasm.

"Mom's blood dripping off the hero's face," Charles says. "Nasty scene."

But it did drip off her face, not only blood but the other stuff too, the other stuff, all over her. Emma knocks the chair back and runs for the bathroom but she doesn't make it. She throws up on the floor beside her dresser. *Dirty girl, dirty little monkey, dirty little puke-face monkey.* Why does he have to see her like this? He'll never love her now. She begins to mop up the vomit with the hem of her shirt. She hears him push back his chair and cross the floor and she mops faster. If she can only get the mess up off the floor, maybe he won't notice. Maybe he didn't see. *Nothing a little soap and water won't erase.*

He puts his hand on her shoulder.

"It's all right, Emma. You go in the bathroom and clean up. I'll take care of this. This always happens at the end."

Later she's lying in bed, facing the wall. She wrote for a little while and then he told her to get into bed. He insisted, for her sake, like someone who loved her, was taking care of her. He took the work she did and sat at the kitchen table with it, scribbling all over her pages. Now he's come over to sit on the edge of the bed. The mattress sags under his weight. Maybe she should get a bigger bed. But for what? He puts his hand on her shoulder and she shudders. Then he lies down beside her and nestles his body against hers, his mouth at her ear.

"I've been thinking," he says softly, running his hand down her arm. "I mean this for your sake, for you, my little girl."

She doesn't like his soft syrupy tone. For her sake? He means it for *her* sake? The motherfucker. She should kill him. He deserves it.

"Everyone gets crazy at the end, Emma. I do; I always have. Those last pages have to be bled out of you." He's stroking her hair. "But you're not in good shape, little girl. You need a rest. I'll take care of you as much as I can, but you need more." His breath is warm against her ear. It's as if he is speaking from inside her head. "You need your family. As soon as you finish, I think you should go and stay for a while with your mother."

Her body goes cold. *Your mother.* As if he knows. As if he knows everything. Her jaw clenches and she starts to grind her teeth. If she had a knife in her hand right now she'd whirl around and stick it in his neck. *Nothing some soap and water won't erase.* She'd stick it in his neck and then she'd laugh and take her book and she'd show him. She'd go to a safe place, *a safe place,* and she'd show him. *And the dirty monkey goes 'round and 'round.*

"Emma?"

She opens her eyes.

"Did you fall asleep?"

"No."

"I was saying I thought you should—"

"I heard you."

"Well?"

"No."

"No?"

"No, I'm not going anywhere. I'm staying here. I'm not going anywhere when I finish the book. I'm staying here and I'm starting a new book. Right away."

He laughs. The mattress shakes beneath them. He puts his arm around her and pulls her body tight against his. She can feel him hard against her ass. "That's the spirit. Ambitious little bitch." He bites her earlobe. "My ambitious little bitch, my little girl."

He grinds against her, his hand sliding her T-shirt up over her ribs. His hand squeezes her ass, biting into her flesh. He's mumbling in her ear—*bitch, dirty little bitch.* He slides his pants down with one hand and then spits into his hand. The spit crackles as he rubs it on himself—*hot little dirty bitch.* He's pressing against her back there, sliding up and down, trying to push in. She doesn't care anymore. She pushes back against him. She wants it. He starts to enter her and a sharp pain cuts through her whole body. Pain. Thank-fucking-God.

She bites his hand and rocks her hips, feeling something slippery back there, as if she's bleeding. Tears are running down her face, but the pain feels so good, so sharp, so hard, pushing everything else out of her mind, she can't stop, she can't stop. There's nothing else now, just this just this. It's like dying, she thinks.

The mother is dead. Zack's mother. Dead and bleeding on the floor of the art room, with the bright-colored paintings on the wall. Gone. That part, the murder, came easily. Charles left the apartment and she sat down at the desk and wrote sentence after sentence with calm precision. She saw the scissors, felt them puncturing flesh again and again and again and again. She won't let Charles change a single word this time.

The sun has moved past the front windows now and Charles still isn't back. She only has a few pages left. It won't take long. The book will end as Zack is entering the cold, echoing halls of the hospital. Emma lays her head down on the wood of the desk and closes her eyes. She'll write the ending in a minute.

Then she feels his hand, shaking her shoulder, shaking her awake. She can smell wet paper under her face—she drooled on her pages.

"Emma," he's saying. "Emma."

Emma, Emma, Emma.

Where is she? How long has she been asleep?

He's saying something to her, but she can't put the words together. "How long have you been asleep?"

How long, how long?

He bends down and brushes her hair off her face. That's when she smells it, smells something, something pretty. She knows that smell. *My pretty powder, not for dirty girls, put it here, dirty girl, between Mommy's pretty legs, nice and soft, doesn't it smell pretty?*

She stands up and pushes back the chair and it topples to the floor. She shoves him away from her. She has enough strength for that. She has enough strength to protect herself.

"Emma!"

She has to get out, out of that filthy apartment above the hardware store, out, away, get to someplace safe. *Some safe place.*

She runs to the door and pulls it open, but he grabs her and drags her back in.

"What are you doing?"

He shakes her, his fingers squeezing her arms, his face on top of hers. She can smell his breath, the hot whiskey smell of his breath, and the powder, the pretty powder. *This is expensive shit, you stupid little freak.* She isn't safe here, she's never been safe here. What is he doing to her?

"Emma! Emma, please. Tell me, tell me. . . ."

She hadn't told him, she hadn't told him—had she? The lamp, the snow, the men who broke down the door, the blood soaking through the little braided rug at the foot of her bed. The powder, the pretty powder. *Violet-scented powder, fifteen bucks a fucking tin.* She hadn't told him about that. How does he know? How does he know about the powder?

"Where did you get it? Where did you get it!"

He slaps her face hard. "Emma. Look at me! Look at me!"

His voice is high and frightened. She has *him* scared now. Good. Why should she be afraid? Why should she? She's defended herself before.

He slaps her again, and blood rushes to her face and her mind slows down. *Slow down, slow down.*

"What are you talking about, Emma? What are you saying?"

It's Charles, Charles, why should she be afraid of Charles?

"Look at me, Emma!"

Sometimes the mind plays tricks on us. Which doctor told her that? Tricky minds. She has a tricky mind. Mommy coming down the hall of the hospital all pretty and bloody, just before dawn. She never could trust her mind. What if she's losing it? Right now, right here, losing her mind. Is there a place where you can find all the lost minds?

"Emma, listen to me, something's happening to you. Can you hear me?"

What does he think? He's shouting in her face. Does he think she's deaf *and* crazy?

"I can hear you," she says, just like a normal person, not shouting, not shouting like him, maybe *he's* the crazy one. "I can hear you perfectly."

He's sweating. She can see it beading up on his forehead. He reaches up and wipes it off. "You had me scared for a moment."

"I did?"

This is easy. You open your mouth and words come out. Easy as taking a step.

"I thought I was losing you for a minute there," he says.

That's funny, she thought she was losing her, too. "I'm fine," she says. "I just need to lie down."

She can talk, she can walk. She walks right past him. Walks right past him and heads toward the bed. One foot in front of the other, easy as can be. Just like that.

And then she collapses.

45

CHARLES LIFTS EMMA into the armchair. Her skin is the color and texture of chalk and her eyes are red-rimmed, their lids heavy. Her breathing is shallow, a plaintive little sigh accompanies each exhalation. He has to get her to the hospital. Quickly. He wraps his jacket around her and lifts her in his arms. As he carries her down the stairs, he realizes how much weight she's lost; she's nothing but skin and bones.

Outside, he hails a cab and gently helps her into it.

"Park Square Hospital," he tells the driver.

It's one of the best psychiatric hospitals in the city. And certainly the most discreet. Tucked away on a side street in the East Fifties, the six-story limestone building looks more like an expensive apartment house than a hospital. Several of Charles's friends have used it as a place to dry out or cool down, and Dan Leber, considered one of the most progressive psychiatrists in the country, is second-in-command. Charles wants Emma to have the best care.

He helps her out of the cab and into the building. The lobby is quiet and clean, and there's a carpeted lounge with a fireplace. Charles leads Emma into the lounge and sits her down in a deep wing chair. He walks over to the admitting desk and speaks to the calm, concerned nurse. She picks up the phone and speaks quietly.

Moments after she hangs up, Dan Leber appears in the lobby, looking grave and professional. He greets Charles and then leads him to a quiet alcove.

"She's completely delusional. I'm very worried about her," Charles says.

"Understandably."

"I should have brought her in last week."

"Don't blame yourself. These things are entirely unpredictable. We'll admit her immediately, and I'll get her started on some stabilizing medication."

Charles sighs heavily. "Christ."

"Charles, I'm sure your concern means a great deal to her. But the fact is, she's not your responsibility. I'll check into state hospitals near her family."

Emma doesn't know where she is. The chair and the carpet are soft and cozy. And the music is soothing. Is it the Beatles? Her father loved the Beatles. "Strawberry Fields Forever." Is she in a safe place? The room has a fireplace with a real fake fire. The colors are pretty. She's so tired. She lays her head against the back of the chair and pulls Charles's jacket around her. It's so soft. What's in the pocket? Something heavy is weighing it down. Is it a gun? She hopes it's a gun. She feels it. No, it's only his keys. Too bad. But won't he need them? Where is he, anyway? He was just here, with her. He can't go home; he won't be able to get in. She has to find him, give him his keys. She lifts them out of the pocket. There's something else. Some money. And a matchbook. It has writing on it: "Hearty Home Cooking, Terrace Diner, Munsonville, PA."

That's funny. She's from Munsonville and so are the matches.

What a small world. She's even been to the Terrace Diner. Running away, she'd been running away. But she'd had no money and they found her hiding in the bathroom and they called her mother and she got the living shit kicked out of her. She doesn't like that diner. She doesn't want these matches. She'll give them back to him, back to Charles. *Running away, I'm running away.* But how did he get them? Why are they in his jacket? *"Do you think Zack had fish?"* The matches, from Munsonville, in *his* jacket. *Pretty powder, pretty powder.* The apartment, that apartment that smells like grease and damp and hate. That apartment where her mother lived, her sick sad mother. *Running away, I'm running away.*

Dan Leber leads Charles back toward the lounge.

"By the way, after the memorial I started rereading *Life and Liberty*. Extraordinary," the doctor says.

"Thank you."

"We'll do our best for the girl."

They round a corner and the lounge comes into view. Emma is gone.

Emma is running down the street. She doesn't know where to go. There is no safe place. The tall buildings are closing in on her, they might fall—don't look up, don't look up. She could run to the bus station and get on a bus. But to where, to where? The city is so big, and nobody cares about one crazy little girl all alone. California! She'll go to California, she'll find her father, she'll find him, and everything will be all right. Her father loves her, he loves her. "Teach your children well . . . and know they love you." But first she has to get Zack, she has to get her book, it's *her* book, not his. *It's in a safe place.* She'll get her book and run away to California and find her father because he loves her and then everything will be all right. Good plan, good girl good girl. Now get your book, get your book and run. *Running away, I'm running away.*

Emma sits up straight in the back of the cab, like a rich lady. She brushes the hair out of her face. She's fine. Everything is working out. She has to move quickly, though, she can see that now. She can't trust him. Only her father. She can trust her father. He probably lives in a little cottage in Santa Cruz. They have a boardwalk there, with a roller coaster and a Ferris wheel. When he sees her he'll cry. He'll make her corn bread like he used to when she was a little girl, before she was a dirty monkey. *Dirty monkey, dirty monkey.* Emma pinches the skin on her wrist as hard as she can, digs her nails in. It helps her to stay calm. When she stops there's a half-moon of blood. Her blood.

The doorman opens the taxi door. Emma smiles at him as she gets out. "I'm on an errand for Mr. Davis," she says. Her voice sounds normal. Why shouldn't it? She's just coming to get her book; nothing crazy about that. She crosses the lobby with slow, measured steps and presses the button for the elevator. She can tell the doorman is watching her. That's all right. She's cool. She just looks straight ahead. At the wallpaper. It has little fleurs-de-lis on it. Or are those bugs?

The elevator doors open and Emma runs down the corridor. It's hard to get the key in the lock because her fingers are trembling. That's strange; she isn't nervous. But she has to hurry, her daddy is waiting and he has corn bread in the oven. She grabs her wrist with her other hand and steadies herself. She gets the key in. She steps into the foyer and stands perfectly still, listening. The apartment is so big and so empty and so quiet. She picks up a vase and throws it against the wall.

She runs through the kitchen, down the long hallway and into Charles's office. *Running away, I'm running away like my daddy did, to California.* She throws open the drawers of his desk and paws through the contents, throwing things all over the room. The last drawer is locked and none of the keys fit. She runs back to the kitchen and grabs a heavy knife from a wooden block. The knife feels good in her palm, it has real heft, she could kill someone with it. If *he* shows up, she'll kill him. Like Zack killed his mother. *Stab him again and again and again.* She slides the knife into the top of the drawer and jabs again and again and again—the lock gives. There's a neat stack of papers in the drawer. Her manuscript, her book. Except her name isn't on it. His name is: *The Sky Is Falling* by Charles Davis.

How stupid of him, to put his name on her book. Does he really think he can get away with it? Her daddy is going to be so mad at Charles because her daddy loves her. He might come all the way east and beat him up because he hurt Emma and Daddy doesn't let anybody hurt Emma. *Daddy, Mommy's hurting me, Daddy.* But it doesn't matter anyway, because she's running away now, with her book. *Running away, I'm running away.* Emma lets the knife drop from her hand. She lifts the manuscript from the drawer and slides it into a soft canvas briefcase. She looks around the room. Such a pretty room. She spent so many hours here, with Charles. One afternoon they made love on that couch. It's all messy now, with blankets. Maybe she should lie down, just for a minute. And Charles will come and lie beside her and hold her in his arms. No, that isn't a good idea. Maybe if her daddy wasn't waiting. He wants to take her on the Ferris wheel. From the tippy-top you can see all the way to China.

Emma smiles at the doorman. She feels better now. She even pats the briefcase. "I got what I came for," she says. Now she can go to California before the corn bread gets cold. She walks out onto Central Park West. *California I'm a-coming home.*

"Hello, Emma."

Charles is there. Where did he come from? She has to ignore him. She doesn't want a scene. Not right here in front of his building. Plus it's her book, and he doesn't seem to understand that. She cradles the briefcase to her chest and crosses Central Park

West. Charles follows, walking right beside her. Emma just keeps walking. She enters Central Park. Charles follows. A light rain begins to fall.

"What do you think you're doing, Emma?"

"You want to steal it," she says. There, that should shut him up. Show him she's no fool. He'd better stop following her. She wishes she'd brought the knife with her. She could stick it into him and really shut him up.

She keeps walking, quickly. In the playground, mothers are gathering up their children and heading home. There's a little black girl sitting alone in a sandbox, crying. Where is her mommy? *Run away, little girl, run away.*

Emma clutches the book, *her* book, tightly. She has to keep walking. She'll be safe if she just keeps walking.

"Emma, that's the finest hospital in the city. They were going to help you."

Don't look at him, don't look don't look.

Emma crosses the park drive. The path splits in two. Which one should she take? She can't stop, stopping would be the worst thing she could do. She bears left and quickens her pace. The path winds up a hill, grows narrower, and is crowded with trees. Suddenly there are no people around. It's dark on the path and the rain is coming down harder. Emma walks faster.

"You don't belong in New York, Emma, you're too fragile."

Don't listen don't listen don't listen.

"No one's going to believe you wrote that book. A girl with your problems."

Emma feels the cold rain soaking through her clothes. It's so dark on the path. Ahead of her it opens up, there's light. She has to get there, she'll be safe there, there will be people there. Her daddy will be there and he'll save her from her mommy and Charles and all the people who want to hurt her.

Emma runs and suddenly the path opens into wide steps and she runs up the steps and she's high up, in a courtyard beside an old stone castle. It's a beautiful place, up above the world. He brought her here once, a long long time ago. They leaned against the wall and looked all the way to Harlem. She looks around wildly. Where is her daddy? He isn't here. *Daddy, please come, Daddy, please come, Mommy's hurting me.*

"Emma, you need help. You didn't have to kill your mother. You could have gotten help. You could have run away, but you didn't."

How can he say that to her, how can he? Doesn't he understand? She didn't want to kill her mother, she *had* to, she had to. She loved her mother, she loved her so much, she was her mommy. They made paintings together, with their fingers. *Pretty painting, Mommy, pretty painting.* Her mommy told her funny stories and they sang silly songs and painted with their fingers and then Daddy came home and made corn bread. *I love you, Mommy, I love you.* He shouldn't say that to her, he shouldn't. She'll show him, she'll show him what *she* knows. She reaches into the pocket of his jacket and pulls out the matchbook and throws it at him. *There, Charles, what do you think of that?* Then she starts to cry.

"You never loved me . . . you only wanted my book. That's all you ever wanted."

Charles looks down at the soggy matchbook and up at Emma. He sees her sobbing, shaking body, the hair matted across her cheek, her hands held like claws. He's never seen anyone so lost. So hopelessly lost. Like a small wounded animal abandoned by its mother, all alone in the woods with night falling. And the rain pelting down.

But she's wrong about one thing: he did love her.

His face changes. She sees it. Something lifts in his eyes. His mouth softens.

"I'm sorry," he says. "I want to hold you." Is he crying too, or is that the rain?

He moves toward her, slowly, and then he has his arms out and is almost touching her. *Mommy has her arms out and Daddy is making corn bread.*

She blinks through the rain and her tears and Charles is beside her.

"I do love you, Emma."

He looks like a little boy who's lost his mommy. Like I lost my mommy. Like I lose everything.

"I've done terrible things, Emma. Please don't hate me."

"I don't hate you."

Thunder rolls across the sky and she lets the book slip from her grasp; she doesn't care about it anymore, it doesn't matter—it has only brought her this.

She runs her trembling hand down Charles's cheek. She wants to comfort him, say something gentle and tender—*little lost boy, poor Zack*—but there's no time. *Running away, I'm running away, Daddy's waiting, I can't be late. California I'm a-coming home.* Still, she wants her last words before she leaves to be words of kindness.

"I love you," she says. And then she turns, pulls herself up to the top of the wall, and jumps.

46

MARK AND JUDY NEALY of Medford, Massachusetts, checked into the Stanhope Hotel at 10:45 last night, which happened to be their wedding night. Their fourteenth-floor suite has a view of Central Park, just as they requested. Except for a cursory hour spent, at Judy's insistence, at the Metropolitan Museum of Art, they've stayed in bed the entire day. They're looking forward to seeing *Ragtime* tonight.

It's just past four o'clock in the afternoon when Mark Nealy, a software engineer, gets up from the bed, puts on the thick terry-cloth robe that the hotel provides, and goes to the window. He's sure about the time because Judy has just turned on *The Oprah Winfrey Show*. Harrison Ford is the scheduled guest, and Judy jokes that she married Mark only because of his resemblance to her favorite movie star.

It's hard to see much through the driving rain, but the gray turret of Belvedere Castle is clearly visible. The castle sits on a rock ledge above a small lake and the Delacorte Theatre, an outdoor stage where Shakespeare plays are performed during the summer. Then Mark makes out two people, a man and a woman, in the courtyard beside the castle. How strange to be out in this weather, he thinks—but hey, this is New York.

He watches as the woman reaches up and touches the man's face. Then she turns and climbs up on the wall that encloses the courtyard and throws herself off. The man reaches out to save her, but it's too late. Her body lands beside the lake, on a flat slab of rock.

47

IT'S A SUMMER NIGHT, a night filled with perfume and hope and youth. New York is a twenty-first-century dream, all light and movement racing fearlessly toward the future.

The party, at the River Café, is the hottest ticket in town. As well it might be. *The Sky Is Falling* has been the beneficiary of a carefully orchestrated publicity campaign. The world loves a comeback and Charles Davis is making one of the biggest. The book is being hailed as brilliant, revelatory. Critics are calling it original, wrenching, with the grim inevitability of tragedy—and then the startling ending, hope snatched from the jaws of horror. The final image is of Zack and his aunt, watching the sunset from her front porch. He's safe and loved. Saved.

Charles's triumph is tempered only by the fact that Portia and Emma aren't alive to share it with him. Emma was so important to the book; her story inspired it. If only her ending could have been as serene as Zack's. The publicity surrounding his gallant attempt to save her was the beginning of his career resurrection. Even the whispers of an affair only add to his reputation. How bitterly ironic it all is. The only solace Charles can take is in the book's dedication: "In memory of a lovely lost child." He thinks of it as Emma's book as much as his own.

Charles, after a long run, is getting dressed for the party. Anne must be down in Eliza's nursery, the former guest bedroom. So much about the apartment has changed in the last couple of months. As part of a clean break with the past, Charles has moved his office to a studio on Riverside Drive. Anne is knocking down the walls between the two rooms of his old workspace, creating a bright and sunny bedroom for their daughter. Things have been going so well between them; their lives are back on track, running smoothly. He's so lucky to have her, taking care of things, turning chaos into order. Those months with Emma were frightening— Charles feels as if he came to the very edge of madness, peered into the abyss. But now he's back, safe and sound, nurtured by Anne.

She's in an incredibly up mood; he hasn't seen her this happy in months, maybe years. It's the baby, of course, but also his triumph. She's been so supportive during the whole ordeal. He's going to be a wonderful husband—and father—from now on. It's time to buy a country place, maybe up on the Hudson.

Anne is leaning over the crib, tickling Eliza's perfect tiny tummy, and her daughter is laughing, looking up at her mother, her eyes filled with recognition and love. Anne strokes her silky red hair— so much for beach vacations. She's enthralled by her baby—by her fingers and toes, by the way she feels and smells and moves, by the noises she makes and the grave intelligence in her eyes. Anne takes her to the office every day, can hardly bear to be away from her.

Her phone rings.

"Hello?"

"Hello, darling."

"Hi, Mother."

"I'm so excited about this party. Wait until you see what I'm wearing."

"Tell me now."

"DKNY jumpsuit. All black. Am I hip or what?"

"You're hip."

"You sound terrific, Anne."

"I'm in love," Anne says, looking down at Eliza.

"John Farnsworth tells me your profits have zoomed."

"They've zoomed so much that I won't be needing him much longer. It's a pity he and Marnie couldn't make it down for the party."

"They're keeping a very low profile."

"I'm not surprised," Anne murmurs.

"The dedication ceremony at the Museum of Fine Arts was *agony* for them. The story of John forcing himself on that business-woman was splashed all over the front page of the *Boston Herald* that very day. They both kept up appearances, but the occasion was ruined."

Kayla's friend, professional that she is, has sent Anne a copy of the *Herald*. She was tempted to frame it. Revenge cost her twenty thousand dollars, but would have been a bargain at twice the price.

"I'm so sorry I couldn't be there to support them," Anne says.

"The woman wanted him to finance her company and he insisted on sex. Right there in her suite at the Four Seasons! She apparently tape-records all her business meetings. Smart girl. John's language on the transcript was terribly crude. Did he think she was some kind of glorified prostitute or something?"

"You'd think John of all people would know that business is business."

"Exactly. It's going to be a while before he can show his face in public. Poor Marnie."

"Poor Marnie," Anne agrees.

"I better go hurry Dwight along. See you soon, darling."

"Good-bye, Mother."

Anne reaches down into the crib and Eliza grabs her forefinger. "You've got a strong grip there, young lady." Eliza giggles with delight.

Charles puts on his jacket and smiles into the mirror. Yesterday, Norman fucking Mailer called to tell him how fine the book is. He's going to get a good run out of this one. A good run.

The in-house phone rings.

"Yes?"

"Your limousine is here, Mr. Davis."

"Thank you."

Where is Anne? It's virtually impossible to pry her away from that child. She's even been sleeping in the nursery. New mothers.

"Anne, the car is downstairs," Charles calls from the doorway.

Anne walks out of the nursery—wearing jeans and a T-shirt.

"You're not dressed," he says.

"I'm sorry," Anne says calmly. "Eliza and I were deep in conversation."

"How is it you two find so much to talk about?"

"We have a lot in common."

There's an edge in her voice. That's all right, he has to expect these little waves of resentment to wash in every once in a while. Anne's done a remarkably good job of forgiving, but he knows it's going to take a while for her to forget. He follows her as she walks into the bedroom.

"The car is downstairs, Anne. We're running late. You're going to have to do a quick change."

She smiles at him humorlessly and says, "I'm not planning to change."

"Oh? Well, at least no one will accuse you of being over-dressed."

Again, that icy smile of hers. She goes to her bedside table and takes a folder out of the drawer. "The point is, Charles, I'm not going."

"Anne, I know how hard——"

"I have something here that might interest you," she says.

What the hell is all this about?

"When I was supervising the packing up of your office, I found these pages in Emma's bottom desk drawer. They were tucked away under some old magazines. It was almost as if she had hidden them there."

Anne crosses to Charles and opens the folder in front of him. She begins to leaf through manuscript pages of *The Sky Is Falling*. The margins are heavily scribbled with notes to Emma in Charles's handwriting.

Charles hears a ringing in his ears; his mouth goes dry.

"So interesting, to see a work in progress," Anne says. She closes the folder and hands it to him. "You might want to save these for your archive at Dartmouth. I have lots more."

"More?"

"Yes. In a safe deposit box. My lawyer has the key."

Charles opens the file and looks down at a page. There's a streak of smudged ash—Emma was smoking when she read his notes. Emma.

Anne goes and sits on her side of the bed. Charles stands absolutely still, the open folder in his hand. He looks so stupid—and he's such a smart man.

"I'm divorcing you, Charles, and I'm getting full custody of Eliza. You won't see her, or me, again. When you walk out of this apartment tonight, you're never coming back."

Charles opens his mouth to speak, but it takes several moments for him to form the words.

"Anne, please . . ."

"I'm letting you have the book, Charles. Don't push your luck."

"It's the process," he manages. "We worked together."

"That's bullshit and you know it. You stole that book. I'd like nothing more than to expose you for who you really are. But then my life—and Eliza's—would be tainted too, wouldn't they? I can't let that happen."

Charles has gone as slack as a rag doll.

"You'd better hurry. The car is downstairs, remember? Everyone's waiting for you."

Still he doesn't move. She goes to him and straightens his tie.

"Don't look so grim, Charles. I'm sure it's going to be a wonderful party."

Liz Smith

Just a year after her high-profile divorce, **Anne Turner** has landed squarely on her feet. PrimeTime Cable Network announced yesterday that the carrot-topped dynamo will be adding a television studio to her stunning new headquarters building—she's been inked by the network to develop and run You're Home, a new cable channel devoted to "the fine art of living." Anne's comment on the latest exploits of her ex-husband was a generous "No comment." Fans of the brilliantly gifted **Charles Davis** were saddened by news of his arrest last week on drunk driving charges in western Pennsylvania.

ABOUT THE AUTHOR

Sebastian Stuart is a native New Yorker who now lives in Cambridge,
Massachusetts. *The Mentor* is his first novel.